PICO STREET STORIES

PICO STREET STORIES

&

The Fortunes of Pedro

By

Kingsley Tufts

JOHN DANIEL & COMPANY
SANTA BARBARA, CALIFORNIA
1998

Published by John Daniel & Company
A division of Daniel and Daniel, Publishers, Inc.
Post Office Box 21922
Santa Barbara, CA 93121

LIBRARY OF CONGRESS CATALOGING-IN-PUBLICATION DATA
Tufts, Kingsley
    [Pico Street stories & The Fortunes of Pedro]
    Pico Street stories / by Kingsley Tufts.
        p.   cm.
    Originally published as Pico Street stories & The fortunes of Pedro. Los
Angeles, Calif. : K. Tufts, 1984.
    Contents: The fortunes of Pedro — The merry-go-round — Money is
never a gift — A truck for the boss — Murder in the harbor — Something
for nothing — The beautiful bicycle — Invention of the Devil — A night to
remember — The pink angel — A handful of beans.
    ISBN 1-880284-27-8 (alk. paper)
    1. Mexican Americans—California—Social life and customs—Fiction.
I. Title.
PS3570.U38P5   1998
813'.54—dc21   97-37646
                                                      CIP

To

The Saint of this day

CONTENTS

PREFACE

I wrote these stories because I treasure simplicity, tenderness and humor. And I treasure the kindness and goodness of human nature. I admire its inventiveness and ingenuity in the face of adversity. I respect the pride and dignity which are found in the midst of poverty.

Most of these stories first appeared as a series in *The Saturday Evening Post*. They were enjoyed by millions of readers with many requests for a book.

These imaginative stories are simple and timeless. Their characters embody the humanity and frailty of us all. They tell of what we hope and dream and desire. They speak of what we need and value. They were created with great affection and respect. My hope is that they will bring you pleasure.

—Kingsley Tufts

Los Angeles, California

THE FORTUNES OF PEDRO

My father, who is José Gonzalez, often speaks to me of things he wants. "Pedro," he says, "if I had a fine reel like the gringo there, I could put the line out farther and we could catch more fish."

My Uncle Luis, who sits beside him with the grappling hook he has not used all morning, nods his head.

"Someday one will fall into the water," he says hopefully.

It is very well known that many years ago an artist came out to the end of Santa Monica Pier, where we are fishing, and threw his oil paintings into the sea.

My Uncle Luis pulled them out with his grappling hook, and the next day sold them back to the artist for a great sum of money. Since then, my Uncle Luis has not worked but to operate the Gonzalez Salvage Company, which is my Uncle Luis and his grappling hook. "One does not need to know many things," he says.

In June the sun becomes very warm, and Uncle Luis sits with his back to a piling, his hat down on his nose. He and my father have passed the wine bottle back and forth in the paper sack many times before the gringo has come along with the fine reel shining on his pole.

"Hear how quiet she run," my father whispers, as the man makes a long cast. "Not a sound to scare the fish." He pokes me in the ribs. "Ask the gringo how much she cost."

The man wears a new white hat with a screen in it to let in the air. He is very proud of the reel and is afraid I will touch it.

"It's a Ball Starcaster," he says, pointing with a white finger to the end, "and it has the star drag. See? Comes with two spools that can be interchanged."

"How much?"

He scratches his chin. "I don't remember," he says, "but I think twelve dollars."

Because the idea has come to me, I say, "I am going to get such a reel for my father on his birthday."

The man smiles, and I am glad I have said it. "You couldn't do better," he says. "Just ask for the 'Ball Six Hundred.' They're scarce, but you may find one."

I thank him and go back to my father.

"Twelve dollars."

"That is not too much," my father says. "It has a blue knob on the handle. It would soon pay for itself."

My Uncle Luis grunts. "One does not hook the fish with the reel."

"With the guitar you do not kiss Rosa Gomez either," my father laughs, "but it helps."

"It is her guitar," Uncle Luis yawns. "Besides, it is not needed."

I have made up my mind to buy the reel for my father on his birthday. All that is lacking is the twelve dollars. In the night, while my Uncle Luis and my father are snoring, I think a great deal about this thing. *In the morning,* I say to myself, *I will go to Mr. Pasquales' tackle store and see if such a reel is to be had.* Mr. Pasquales is not my friend, but I have bought a few hooks from him in the past and his store is well known to me through the glass window.

In the morning while we are drinking our coffee, I decide to say nothing of my desire to make the present to my father until I have been to see Mr. Pasquales.

"Pedro, what day is she today?" my Uncle Luis asks.

My father laughs into his saucer of coffee as Uncle Luis looks to the wall where is hung the calendar we get free from the fish store at Christmastime. On the calendar is marked with a red fish all the fast days. In fine print under the numbers is the name of the saint for each day.

"Today is June third. Saint Clotilda's Day, Uncle Luis."

"Saint who?"

"Saint Clotilda."

"That one, she's a funny one!" he says, repeating it after me. When he has stretched himself and rolled a cigarette, he starts for Manuel Velez's barbershop, where he hears the news on the radio, and I walk with him.

There is much sun in the barbershop and it is warm. "Today is Saint Clotilda's Day!" he says as he goes in. "She's a fine day for feeling good!" The others make a place for him. At home they have the calendar free from the fish store, too, but they do not see its importance as Uncle Luis does.

At the tackle store, Mr. Pasquales is wrapping the dead sardines with salt in newspapers. For a little package of such poor bait he charges ten cents.

"Good morning, Mr. Pasquales," I say. "Today is Saint Clotilda's Day! It is a fine day for feeling good!"

"Huh?" he says, looking down at me. "When I am a little boy like you, every day she's a good day. What you want?"

"Do you have a fishing reel that is called the 'Ball Six Hundred'? That is a Starcaster with a blue knob on the handle?"

Mr. Pasquales looks at me like I am coo-coo. "That is no reel for a little boy like you."

"I am making a present to my father for his birthday," I say proudly.

"So?" he says. "How is your father called? When is this birthday?"

"José Gonzalez. The twenty-fourth of this month, the day of Saint John the Baptist," I reply, for I have read it from the calendar only this morning.

"Smart little feller, huh? Maybe someday you will be a priest, no?"

"No," I answer. "My Uncle Luis is going to take me into his salvage business."

"Luis Gonzalez?"

"Yes, sir."

Mr. Pasquales puts his arms on the glass case and laughs at me. "What are you called?" he asks.

"Pedro."

"Pedro, where did you steal the money for this fishing reel?"

"I did not steal it!" I cry.

He shrugs his shoulders. "What's a difference? How much you got?"

"You have such a reel?"

"But of course," he says. "Only one, and there is no other to be had." He reaches behind him on the shelf and takes down a box. "See," he says, "she's a beaut! She's a dandy!"

It is just such a one as the gringo had, with a blue knob on the handle. "Two spools?" I ask.

Mr. Pasquales looks in the box. "Two spools," he says.

"Twelve dollars?"

"Twelve dollars an' two bits tax. You want I should wrap him up?"

I shake my head. "I have not that much money. Please, Mr. Pasquales, will you keep this reel for me?"

He looks at me with disgust and puts the lid on the box. "How long should I keep him?"

"Until my father's birthday. That is only three weeks."

He does not like this. "How much money you got? Pull him out; maybe we make a deal."

I am very sad. "Mr. Pasquales, I do not want to take the reel; I only want you should keep it for me."

"How much you got?"

He cannot be argued with. "None," I admit, adding quickly, "but I will earn this money and bring it to you."

He throws up his hands, grabs the box and sticks it back on the shelf. "How you get this money?" he asks angrily. "You never see twelve dollar in your life."

"I will sift sand on the beach and find money," I say. "People lose much money."

He glares at me.

"I will pick up bottles on the beach. There are many bottles."

He snorts and shakes his head.

"I will cut people's lawns," I say finally.

"Without a lawn mower?"

"Why not?" I ask. "My father has no lawn mower and he cuts many lawns."

"Get out!" he says. "Come back when you have the money. If the reel she's here, I sell her to you." He slaps more sardines in the newspapers, and that means he is through with me.

I do not go home, but think I must begin at once to earn this money. In the alley behind the eating places along the walk by the beach, I find a paper sack with handles on it, and go out on the sand to pick up bottles.

These I will sell for two cents apiece to Carmelita Smith at the hamburger stand by the merry-go-round. I am well known to her through my Uncle Luis, and it is not far to walk. There are many people on the beach, and this first day I pick up ninety-four bottles, which is a dollar eighty-eight cents.

When I arrive home, my father is at the stove frying a fish in the pan, and Uncle Luis is drinking wine from the gallon bottle on the table. I listen to the talk while I am thinking of a place to put the dollar eighty-eight cents, which I am afraid will be heard in my pocket.

"But I need a lawn mower," my father is saying. "These people do not keep the blades sharp in their machines."

"It is a heavy thing," Uncle Luis says. "You would need a truck to haul it around."

"A little wagon that you pull would be enough," my father answers.

Uncle Luis shakes his head. "People would want to borrow these things, and either you could not work or you would lose your friends."

"There is something in what you say," my father admits as he studies the skillet.

"Don't burn the fish," Uncle Luis says.

"I am not my own boss," my father goes on.

"You would work for the machine," Uncle Luis says flat to him. "You would have to take care of it every day, like you have to wind a watch."

"Quick, Pedro," my father says, "bring the plates."

"A halibut," Uncle Luis smiles at me. "For showing a gringo how to clean a mackerel, he gives me a halibut."

"Luis tell him the halibut she got worms this time of year." My father winks.

"Where have you been today, Pedro?" Uncle Luis asks.

"Watching the steam shovels where the new store is going to be."

"Good," he nods. "One learns much by watching."

In the evening when we are sitting on the bench by the door, smoking, I say, "I am going to the beach. Perhaps someone has left a sweater on the sand."

"Rosa's guitar needs tuning," says Uncle Luis, yawning. "When the fish is settled, I will go to her house."

My father says nothing. He is looking through the cigarette smoke to the red geranium growing in the rusty can. "I do not know which I want more," he says, "a machine to cut grass or a fine reel like the gringo had."

I borrow the sand sifter, which is a wire scoop on a handle, from the lifeguard station, saying I have lost a pocketknife. I sift by the wall where the women sit to watch the kids. Before it is dark I have found eighty cents, two lipsticks, a false tooth, and filled my pockets with good cigarette butts.

When I come home, my father is sleeping with his shoes on, and Uncle Luis is not yet returned. The cigarette butts I put in the can on the table for us tomorrow, and while I take off my father's shoes, I think of where to put my money, which is now two dollars sixty-eight cents this first day. I think of Mr. Pasquales with a sneer in my heart; it is so easy to get this money. With a pin, I open the sand blister on my foot and let out the water. Then I go outside by the steps and put the money under the rusty geranium can. No one has ever moved this can, as it was placed there by the father of Rosa Gomez, who owns this house.

Because I cannot decide to tell my Uncle Luis what is in my mind, it is necessary for me to be careful. It is often necessary to fish all day or to watch the steam shovel. But every day I go to Mr. Pasquales' tackle store to look at the reel.

It is a week from my father's birthday when Mr. Pasquales asks one morning, "Pedro, how much dough you got now?"

"Eight dollars."

"Show me these dollars," he says.

But I shake my head. "It is in a safe place."

"I'll bet it is!" he laughs. "How much you make yesterday?"

"Nothing. Yesterday I help my father pull devil grass from a lawn."

"You work today?" he asks.

I nod. "Monday is very good. From Sunday many bottles are left on the sand."

"What is the saint of this day?" he asks to catch me.

"Saint Adolph."

"You good little boy," he says. "I think you got a good mamma."

"No," I answer.

"No mamma?"

"No."

"In the good heaven she is taking care of little Pedro." He pats my head.

"She went to Salinas," I answer, "with a lettuce picker from Imperial Valley."

Mr. Pasquales scratches his neck as he watches me from the door. If he did not have a reel to sell, I think he would be my friend.

In the evening there is a chill in the air and we are sitting by a small fire of milk cartons which are saved for us at the drugstore. I would be very happy thinking of the nine dollars eighty-five cents I now have under the geranium can if Uncle Luis did not look at me so closely.

"Did I not see you on the beach today?" he asks.

"Maybe," I admit to him. "I went swimming."

"With a sackful of bottles?"

"I was very hungry after the swim. I pick up a few bottles to sell for a hamburger."

"Carmelita says you bring bottles every day."

"That is true. Every day I am hungry."

"There is much money in the sale of bottles," Uncle Luis says, after a little while.

"Fernando Gomez built his junk yard starting from bottles," my father adds. "And from the junk yard he has many houses to rent, like this one."

"Fernando Gomez is a weak man, but honest," Uncle Luis says, squinting at me. "It is known to all that he cannot resist the temptation to save money. It is no secret."

"Someday he will leave it to Rosa," my father says pleasantly.

"That is not to the point," Uncle Luis replies. "It is money under the boards of a house or hid in a sand hole that is bad."

"One should give bad money to the church," my father says; "then it will not trouble him."

"Or spend it to a good purpose," I add.

"That is true," Uncle Luis says, "but to buy a thing which will be a burden is not to spend it to good purpose."

I return his look with great innocence, and he sits heavy and sad in his chair.

"I am going down to watch through the door at the dance hall," I say.

Uncle Luis squashes his cigarette butt under the edge of the table. "I have had a long talk with Juan Pasquales at the tackle store today," he says. "He thinks you are a nice little boy."

"Me?" I answer, and my heart flops in my shirt like a small mackerel.

Uncle Luis nods. "He tell me all about you."

"What does he say?" my father asks.

Uncle Luis gives me a look that says he will not tell all he knows. "Pasquales say Pedro know all the saints' days."

"Pasquales is smart. He has a good business," my father answers. "He saved his money."

Uncle Luis grunts. "Pasquales is dumb. He works all day, so his wife gives the money to Manuel Velez for to make her pretty. Then she goes to Gardena with Jesús Rinaldo. Maybe some night Pasquales wake up and kill Rinaldo."

Seeing the talk is going another way, I start for the door.

"You fish with me tomorrow?" Uncle Luis asks.

I know he wants to speak about the money, so I say, "I am going to Redondo Beach to look for moonstones."

"That is too bad." He is full of disappointment. "I have seen some fine starfish on the pilings today. We could bring them up with the hook."

"I am going to Redondo," I repeat. "If I find a good stone, I will sell it and bring home a chicken."

"There is no hurry," Uncle Luis says.

Outside, I go to the dance hall and walk up and down by the door, my hands in my pockets, listening to the music and worrying about my money. Uncle Luis knows how much I have, if Pasquales told him. Tomorrow, if I go to Redondo and my father is cutting lawns, Uncle Luis will take the house to pieces to find it. I conclude it is not safe to leave the money under the geranium can, and yet I cannot think of a better place.

When I return home, the wine bottle is upset on the floor. Uncle Luis and my father are asleep, and I reason that perhaps tomorrow Uncle Luis will not feel like turning things upside down to look for the money.

In the morning I do not wait for them to wake up, but find my breakfast in the boxes behind the Drive-In on Lincoln Boulevard. When a truck driver sees me digging in the box, he becomes sorry and buys a good breakfast of ham and eggs for me. It is on his truck, which is going to San Pedro, that I ride to Redondo Beach.

It is a lucky day for me. I find many moonstones and bottles, and sell them without trouble. I am rewarded with a dollar for a dog which has become lost and is following me. It was nothing, because the street address was on his collar, and we are almost there when I find him. On the pier I beg a three-pound halibut from a gringo who has caught fish only for fun, and this I sell to a little restaurant for another dollar, which is like giving it away. After buying pop and a hamburger, in my pocket now are four dollars, and the fine fishing reel for my father is in the bag with a dollar sixty to spare.

On the way to the highway, a silly chicken becomes frightened of me and flies into the way of an automobile. The woman who is driving the car takes the chicken and me to the highway, where I say I am meeting my mother, who is coming on the bus from San Pedro. Because she is sorry about the chicken, she gives me fifty cents, and when the bus comes, I get on and ride with the chicken home to Santa Monica. All the way home I try to think of the saint's name who watches over this day, until I remember that I did not read the calendar in the morning. But I decide, anyway, he is the best saint for a long time.

It is not yet dark when I walk down Pico Street from the bus stop.

Rose Gomez calls to me from the office of the junk yard. "Come to supper tonight, Pedro! Bring the chicken!"

And at Manuel Velez's barbershop they laugh and call out to run, that I am followed by a cop. Everybody is glad that there is a chicken for me and my father and Uncle Luis.

When I see our house, there is no smoke from the pipe at the side, and it is very quiet. The door is standing open.

"Papa José!" I call from the walk. "Uncle Luis! I have brought a chicken!"

There is no answer.

Inside, on the floor, my father is lying, his face under the bed. A quart of whisky which is almost gone is on the floor by the leg of the table. There is no Uncle Luis.

"Pedro, bring the flashlight!" my father is saying under the bed. "I think I kill my brother!" He is so drunk he is talking crazy.

"Where did you get this whisky?" I shake him. "Where is Uncle Luis?" But he is saying only that Uncle Luis is chopped up in the lawn mower under the bed.

"Where does the money for so much whisky come from?" I cry to myself, and then I am afraid to look. I run outside to the geranium can and lift it easy to one side.

It is gone. The money is gone. "My father has stolen it from me!" I cry. I run back inside. Because I am still holding it, I beat my father with the dead chicken, and sit down in the feathers to cry. "You do not deserve to have the reel," I say to him. "You are a dirty thief."

When my Uncle Luis comes in the door, he holds on to a chair and looks at me.

"That is a fine chicken," he says.

"You can have it," I answer, and kick it along the floor to him.

"I will start the fire," he says. "Put some coffee in the pot. When the water is hot, I will clean and pick this chicken."

I cannot believe my ears. I have never seen him pick a chicken before.

"My father is a pig!" I say. "He stole my money!"

"Do not speak ill of your father," Uncle Luis answers carefully. "Money is a great curse."

"I did not think he would do such a thing," I say bitterly.

"You should not have tempted your father with this money."

"I didn't. It was hid."

"Perhaps you have been careless, and it was impossible not to find it."

"You wanted it yourself!" I accuse him. "Last night you knew I had it!"

"It was only a suspicion," Uncle Luis says. "Pasquales has such a big mouth one must listen."

"But my father beat you to it!" I answer.

He pours steaming coffee into the tin cup. "Put this into Papa José," he says. "He is not used to so much whisky. I will fix the chicken."

As I start to pull my father's legs around, Uncle Luis turns to me. "I would say nothing of this money to him, Pedro. He will be sick enough of this thing as it is."

"Did Mr. Pasquales show you the fishing reel?" I ask.

Uncle Luis is bending over the bucket of hot water with the chicken. He nods.

"It was for his birthday," I say, spilling the coffee into my father's mouth.

"It is a bad thing to live in the future," he answers.

My father opens his eyes and looks at us. A sick smile comes on his face. "Good whisky," he says. "Help me to the bed, Pedro." He sees the blood from the chicken on his hand. "I have been fighting. I have lost much blood."

"Why did you steal my money?" I cry, pushing him on the mattress.

"Steal?" he says. "I steal nothing from you."

"Under the geranium can!" I shake him. "You took my money from under the geranium can!"

He looks at me with blank eyes. "Geranium can?"

"The money!" I cry. "The money for the whisky!"

"Luis bring the whisky," he says, turning over on his face. "There was no geraniums." He is asleep.

I leap to my feet. "You!" I cry at Uncle Luis. "You stole my money!"

He is putting the lid on the skillet, and looks at me with much sorrow. "A man is born to sin, Pedro."

"You did not spend it all for whisky! Where is the rest?"

"It was eaten by the little white mice."

"You lost it! You—you—"

"If I had won with the dice, I would have put the money back," he says. "Besides, there is a lesson to be learned from this."

"I should have known it was not my father."

"You made a mistake," he says.

"Having you for an uncle," I answer.

"No," he says. "I will teach you to be smarter. The next time you move a can with geraniums be careful not to crack the dirt on top. One had but to look to know where the money was."

I say nothing. *There is truth, maybe, in what he says*, I think to myself. *In the dark I have been careless.*

From my pocket I take the four dollars and hold them under his nose. "It is yet five days until my father's birthday, and he will have the reel! You have not told him about this reel, have you?"

He looks at the four dollars and at me. "One who hides his money in more than one place will have no happiness from it. It is a bad thing not to trust people."

"Does he know about the reel?" I ask again.

"No," he answers, "it would have spoiled the whisky."

That night I sleep with the money tied in a rag around my waist, and in the morning I am waiting at the tackle store when Mr. Pasquales arrives.

When we are inside, I look first to see if the reel is still there.

"I want to pay down on the reel," I say, laying four dollars on the glass counter. "If you had not shot your mouth off to Uncle Luis, I could pay it all."

"What's amatter with you?" he asks me.

"Uncle Luis stole nine dollars eighty-five cents from me because you talk too much."

Mr. Pasquales comes out from behind the case, and his red face is turning purple. "Luis Gonzalez steal your money?"

"It's your fault!"

"Where was this money?"

"Under the can of geraniums by the door. He wouldn't have looked for it if you hadn't told him I was saving up."

Mr. Pasquales walks up and down the store. "Dog of a thief," he cries, "to steal from a good little boy!"

"What did you expect," I say, "when you told him I had this money?"

"What you do now?" he asks.

"There is yet five days. I will earn more money." I look at him with much misery. "Will you let me take the reel from the store to show my father on his birthday? Please, Mr. Pasquales! I will bring it back, I promise, until I have paid for it!"

He pats my head. "Sure thing!" he says. "Every day you bring the money to old Pasquales, until there is enough."

As I go out, I hear him swear to work on my Uncle Luis with a fish-cleaning knife if he comes near the store again, and I remember to speak of it when I get home.

"Pasquales has a bad temper," my Uncle Luis says. "Someday he will open his mouth to Jesús Rinaldo and get killed."

Each day I pay over to Mr. Pasquales what I have made and he writes it on a little card. Still, on the morning of my father's birthday, there is yet three dollars ninety cents left to pay. But Mr. Pasquales holds good to his word, and hands the box to me across the glass case.

"I will bring it back this afternoon," I promise.

"Pedro," he says to me then, "I think you pretty good. How you like to work for old Pasquales in this store?"

I am struck dumb. Nobody has asked me such a question before.

"I pay you a dollar every day. If you work for me, the reel, she is yours now, and I take what is owing from the wages. How's about it?"

I want to say yes, but I am afraid. I must speak of this thing with my father and Uncle Luis. I am overcome because Mr. Pasquales will trust me in the store.

"I tell you later!" I cry, rushing to the door. A thought strikes me. I call back breathless. "Be careful of Jesús Rinaldo!" and I am flying up Pico Street to our house.

My father and Uncle Luis are sitting at the table, smoking.

"For you," I say proudly, and hold the box out to my father. "Happy birthday!"

The sun in the window makes it shine like silver when he lifts the reel from the box. "A reel like the gringo's!" He touches the blue knob under the cellophane, and looks at me with so much love I think he will cry. "They will put us in jail," he says finally. "You must take it back."

"No," I answer, with a nasty look at my Uncle Luis. "I did not steal it. I have paid down all but three dollars ninety cents, and Mr. Pasquales is giving me a job in his store for the rest."

"That thing cost twelve dollars," Uncle Luis says, pouring whisky from the bottle into his coffee. "As much as a lawn mower."

My father lays the reel gently on the table. "She is beautiful," he sighs. "With such a reel, one does not need a lawn mower."

"Now you can put the line out a mile!" I exclaim. "Farther than anybody!"

"What line?" Uncle Luis says. "A line for such a reel would cost four dollars."

It is true. The string we have wrapped on our sticks is full of knots and of many sizes. We look at the reel, and there is silence.

"If you work in the tackle store, you could get such a line," Uncle Luis says finally.

"I would have to work four days," I answer, thinking this is a very long time.

"You have worked too much already." My father lifts his eyes from the reel, and there is much goodness in his face.

"One line would not be missed," Uncle Luis says. "Old Pasquales has a shelfful."

"He is my friend!" I say quickly. "I would not take even a hook from him without paying!"

My father nods. "That is right. When one is trusted, his hands are tied." He scratches his ear a little. He is thinking.

It is a bad situation we are against.

"I have a dollar to put on such a line," Uncle Luis says, reaching in his pocket, "but what is the use?" He spins the dollar on the table. "There is no pole. One must have a good pole of split bamboo for such a reel."

"Calcutta bamboo would do," My father says. "Such a pole costs very little."

Uncle Luis returns the dollar to his pocket.

My dollar, I think to myself.

"There is much vanity in these things," Uncle Luis says. "We are warned against false pride."

"But it is not bad to have good tools!" I cry. "To catch more fish is a good thing!"

"Good tools are the ones that get stolen," Uncle Luis points out. "We would not dare to sleep, fishing with such a fine outfit."

"It is true," my father says, but with pride. "We would be envied."

"Worse," Uncle Luis adds, "we would be suspected."

"But we could prove it was paid for," I insist.

Uncle Luis shakes his head. "They would not believe us."

We stare at the reel now, and it does not look so good, until my father lifts it again in his hands. Tears are in his eyes.

Uncle Luis continues, "What would happen at the grocery store? We are given much because it is known we do not have anything. 'If they can pay for a fine fishing outfit,' it would be said, 'they can pay for the meat bones and old bread.' "

But my father has stopped listening. He stands up, holding the reel. His face works until he can speak. "The good God forgive us!" he bursts out. "This is a beautiful thing!"

"But, José—" Uncle Luis opens his mouth.

"Shut up!" my father says. He crosses himself. "I have a confession to make." Taking the bottle from the table, he finishes it in one gulp. His face shines like a church candle. "I have been paying down to Fernando Gomez on a second-hand lawn mower. Ten dollars already. Enough for the line and the pole."

We stare at my father. He has done a hard thing. A wonderful thing. He steadies himself, leaning on the table.

But Uncle Luis sits like a man hit with a lead sinker.

It is like a miracle, I think. *I do not believe it.*

Uncle Luis is reaching in his pocket. He lays the dollar on the table without a sound, shoving it to my father like a last poker chip.

"You will need a bucket for live bait," he says. "You can lower it to the water with the rope from my grappling hook."

"No, Luis," my father says. "I will not take your rope."

"We will divide the fish," Uncle Luis answers.

Suddenly from the porch a guitar is struck. I rush to the door. Outside is Rosa Gomez and old Fernando. Mr. Pasquales is sitting on the steps with Manuel Velez and others from the barbershop. Carmelita Smith is running up the walk. Half of Pico Street has come.

"Chili beans!" she calls, holding out the pot she is carrying.

"Father!" I cry. "Uncle Luis!"

"Happy birthday, José!" They all slap him on the back.

Rosa Gomez has a red rose in her hair, which Uncle Luis smells when he takes the guitar. Everybody is singing.

My father is crying as Manuel Velez holds out a good bottle of Chianti, and Mr. Pasquales presses a small package into his hand.

"A few hooks!" he says, and before I know it, he has me by the arm. "My new man in the store!" he says to everybody. "Pedro Gonzalez! . . . How's about it, José?"

My father nods. "But I do not understand," he manages to say.

Mr. Pasquales shouts above everybody. "Show them the reel, José. They have come to see the reel!"

I know now. Mr. Pasquales has told everybody. The reel for my father's birthday. My father holds it up in the sunlight. It passes from hand to hand. It is a beautiful thing. There are many sighs.

"What it is to have such a son!" old Fernando says, and nods in approval of me.

Jesús Rinaldo passes on the street in his automobile, but Mr. Pasquales is stretched out against a post in the sun, his hands behind his head, watching Carmelita Smith dance on the porch.

Suddenly, with a great smile, he pokes my father, who is sitting in the place of honor with old Fernando on the bench.

"Sure she's a day for to feel good, eh, José?"

My father grips Mr. Pasquales' arm. He nods his head, and then he has to wipe his eyes. He is so happy he can't talk.

THE MERRY-GO-ROUND

It is near Christmas time. There are many long lines at the Pico Street branch of the Bank of Santa Monica when we come out of Señor Andreo's office on this Monday morning.

My daughter, Rosa, and I, Fernando Gomez, are known to all. Everybody waves to us, and it can be seen that each one is scratching his head inside to think what I have been up to with my money. Especially Sam Hondo.

"Let me tell him," Rosa begs. "He will find out anyway."

Sam is standing with the canvas cash sack from his garage, afraid to lose his place in line, but with a big smile for Rosa.

I nod. These two are close to my heart, but farther from each other than is good. From little up, they have tried to outdo each other. They belong to a generation I am not sure I understand.

My Rosa stands only to his shoulder — a red poinsettia to an adobe wall. Sam is big. He has done well fixing automobiles, and is of a good weight from eating in the best restaurants. But when he leans to Rosa, it is with gentleness, and his face spreads to a fine smile as he listens. He looks to me and nods like a happy boy. *It is too bad*, I think, *that my Rosa expects more of a man than is possible.*

"Remember," Sam calls to me now, "I'm a good mechanic. I can fix even a wooden horse."

I see that Rosa is whispering in the line to Chiquita Alvarado, and that Manuel Velez from the barbershop is standing close with big ears.

The sooner the thing is out, the better, I sigh to myself. *After all, one does not buy a merry-go-round every day in the week.*

By the time we are going to the beach in the afternoon, all of Pico Street is shaking its head. At the poultry store, Celita Santee is standing at the counter. "I have made a lot of mistakes in my life," she laughs, "but I never bought a merry-go-round!"

And Juanita Gonzaga, who is a grandmother five times at thirty-eight, leans on her gate and asks if she can ride free with the new baby who is called Gilda.

"Everybody rides free on Christmas!" I say, so all can hear. "There will be a big party!"

The little ones scream from the dirt hole where they are playing at pigs, and fly off in every direction to spread the news.

Señor La Paz, who cuts tombstones and is of my age, nods as we pass.

"I have bought a merry-go-round," I say, thinking it is a thing he would like to turn over in his mind. "They were going to tear it down."

"What?"

"At the beach," I point, "the merry-go-round."

Señor La Paz is quite deaf. "I thought that burned down ten years ago," he says. "Let me show you some good granite for a headstone."

"Come for a free ride on Christmas Day!" I shout in his ear. "Later maybe you can chisel me a stone horse!"

He shakes his head. "That is a week from now. I may be dead. At my age one does not begin a horse."

"You see," I say to Rosa as we go on, "he is criticizing me. He makes himself old on purpose, so a stone horse will be impossible."

I had good reasons for buying this merry-go-round at the Santa Monica beach, but I do not make a noise with them. In the first place, the bank was going to tear it down; it was a losing proposition, without dignity. And in such a case the bank could not think of the little ones. The figures did not show that it is a good thing to begin life riding a horse to music. Which is but a way of coming to my second reason.

I have said to myself that someday, if God permits, I shall have a grandson to ride this merry-go-round. Perhaps a loud organ and jumping horses will bring a change in my Rosa. What I would not say, even in the confession box, is that I have wanted this beautiful thing all my life, and that the money I got from the sale of my junk yard was burning a hole in my pocket.

This merry-go-round is in a pink stucco building shaped like a tent, for which I must pay rent to the bank. Not much, but enough.

There are thirty-six horses, three to the row, and two benches. Also, there is the slotted bar which gives the rings of iron and the one ring of gold, the free-ride ring.

When Rosa and Sam Hondo were children they saved pennies from picking up beans in the bean fields to ride this merry-go-round.

"What a junk heap!" Rosa says now. "Papa, you are back in the same old business."

"New, it cost thirty-five thousand dollars," I say. "All it needs is a little paint."

"And probably a whole new insides," Rosa answers. "Did you look at the insides, papa?"

"It is full of gears and a ten-horse motor," I explain. "The same man has run this machine for fifteen years."

This man, who sees us from his hole in the middle, is called Potsie. He scrambles across the platform on short legs, and his face is a foot long. A sad spider for sure, this one.

"Mr. Gomez?" he asks. When he takes off his hat, there is not a hair to be seen. He is fifty, maybe more.

I nod. "This is my daughter, Rosa Gomez."

He sweeps the ground with his hat. "Señorita, a pleasure!" But his face is dark as a rain barrel. "Mr. Andreo has told me. For me, I guess, it is all over. No?"

He thinks sure I will fire him. "The bank has spoken to me of you," I say. "You like this merry-go-round?"

He makes a smile with a few teeth. "The organ, Mr. Gomez. I love the music."

"You are a musician?"

"I started with a small grinder and a hungry monkey," he says, "but all the time I dream of a big organ." He waves his hand to the horses. "I am in charge of this organ now for many years." He sighs. "It was too good to last."

"What about the machinery?" I ask. "And the tickets? You are in charge of these too?"

He shrugs. "Of course. But one cannot be good at everything."

"You will work for me?" I ask.

He grabs my coat. "Mr. Gomez," he promises, "I will make the organ sing for you like an angel."

"Rosa will take care of the tickets," I instruct, "but this machinery — that is your job too."

He pulls up the pants from his short legs and sticks out his lips. "Then I must tell you," he frowns. "This machinery, she is lousy. If I did not swear at her every minute, she would fall to pieces."

"Swear?" Rosa asks. "In front of the children?"

"Oh, no, señorita!" he says quickly. "Inside. When it is very bad I shut the door."

"I should hope so," Rosa says. "Can't the machinery be fixed?"

Potsie turns up his hands. "The clutch, señorita, the brake, the bearings — where would one start?"

She turns to me. "See, what did I tell you, papa? Sam Hondo will get rich off of us."

"Hondo?" Potsie asks.

"A garageman," I explain, "up on Pico Street."

"Just keep him away from my organ," Potsie says, with a dark face.

"Don't worry," I assure him. "He would not know about an organ."

"All he knows," Rosa says quickly, "is to make money."

I laugh to Potsie. "Sam Hondo is an old friend."

"Who thinks only of business," Rosa observes.

"Come, Potsie," I say then, "make it go around."

When he steps through the horses and rings the bell, it is a fine sound. It is like a motorman starting a streetcar. But when he pushes the lever on the box, the horses tremble like they are shaking off flies.

"Come, Rosa!" I cry. The animals are beginning to jump now. In a second I am on the platform.

"Not on a horse!" Rosa shouts. "On the bench, papa!"

The brass rods move up and down and the music has a fine beat. I cannot stand it. I must ride a horse. With Rosa clinging to me, I climb to the saddle of a white stallion with a black mane. *To ride a horse to music, I think, is to die happy.* Fifteen times we go around, and I am so dizzy I think I will fall off, but I could go again.

"No, papa, no!" Rosa cries in my ear.

Potsie stops the machinery, and I sit in the saddle until the building is no longer moving.

"You see," he says, as he scrambles to us, "she runs like a wash machine full of rocks."

"She is beautiful," I answer. Then I think of what I have forgotten. "The rings!" I laugh and wipe my eyes "I forgot to reach for the gold ring."

"Why you care about that?" Potsie scratches under his hat. "You own this thing."

Because I see he travels with but one gear to his mind, I must explain. "Nobody owns the gold ring," I say gently, "unless it is the saint who watches over it."

His face is an empty dish. "You could be right," he says. "It is the only ring that does not get stolen."

"You see," Rosa says, "an expense."

But I can understand how it is with one of these rings in a small hand. It is smooth and round, and it is something to make up for the gold ring that was missed.

"Wait," Potsie excuses himself. "Customers." He goes to the ticket booth, where two children have come in. With a sigh, he comes to us again. "Waiting for their mamma," he says.

"But maybe now, with Christmas vacation, business will pick up."

I look to the board in the booth where the fare is printed. "Who can ride at such a price?" I say. "That is three pieces of candy! It is too much."

"It was put there by the bank," Potsie shrugs. "That's what it is."

"The bank!" I say with heat. "The bank was going to tear the whole thing down."

"I know," he says. "They wanted to sell me the organ." This is a thing Señor Andreo has not told me.

"And you did not want it?" I ask.

"No, Mr. Gomez!" He pulls his loose pants up higher and buttons his coat.

"You did not have the money," I say. "That was a misfortune."

He looks at me and chews his tongue. "Why shouldn't I tell you?" he says finally. "It happened three months ago. It is not my fault because I did not know until a note was missing."

"Spit it out!" Rosa says. "What's the matter with it?"

He looks away. "She is a beautiful organ; she may play fine for years."

"Come," I help him. "it cannot be so bad."

He is in a corner. He swallows a word. "Termites," he says. "She is lousy with termites."

"Mercy in heaven!" Rosa cries.

"I do not understand," I say. "It plays all right."

"The termites are dead," Potsie answers, "but she is in . . . a very delicate condition." He speaks sadly. "You see, Mr. Gomez, why she must not be touched."

"How long," I ask, "will she last?"

He turns up his hands. "It might come tomorrow; maybe not for six months." He smiles a little to make me feel better. "There is plenty time to fix the clutch and maybe the bearings."

"Yes," I say, "I will see Sam Hondo on the way home."

"What's the use, papa?" Rosa says. "You will only be throwing good money after bad."

"This is a new trouble to you, señorita," Potsie says then, "but not to me. You will get used to it."

"You have told us a hard thing," I say kindly.

"Yes," he nods. "I have told no one else."

"Why didn't you inform the bank?" Rosa accuses him. "Who killed the termites?"

"I did, señorita. Some like this—with my fingernails—some with poison, some with a lighted match. I killed them myself." He turns on his short legs and disappears in his hole in the middle of the machine.

"Who knows?" I say to Rosa. "It may play for years yet."

"We can hope," she answers.

Potsie comes now with a tin can. "See," he says, "dead termites."

Because I must think over what I have seen, I wave the can away, and hit on a small thing for Rosa to do.

"With a rag you could shine the harness on these horses," I say. "And I will go see Sam Hondo."

Potsie stands with his termites. "There is money in the cash box," he says. "What'll I do with it?"

"Give it to Rosa," I say. "We will keep a record," I tell her, "just like the old business."

"I could keep it in my head," she replies, "for all the money we'll see from this thing."

"And you," I say to Potsie, "see that no more termites get into your organ."

I do not stop at Sam Hondo's garage, as I have said, but go home and lie on my bed, making my head empty. For an idea to come, there must be a place for it. It is possible that Fernando Gomez is one who will be remembered for a foolish thing.

It is dark when Rosa wakes me.

"Come, papa," she says. "Eat your supper and tell me what Sam Hondo said."

"I did not see him," I explain. "He is too young to talk to in the afternoon. I went to sleep instead."

There is fish with a good Spanish sauce, but Rosa is without appetite.

"Only seven rides today. Think of that. We must pay the Government tax and that no-good Potsie. We are in the hole already. There is yet the rent and the electricity—" She rattles the coffeepot, and her eyes roll to the ceiling. "Not to mention depreciation . . . and the repairs!"

"The bookkeeping can wait," I say. "It is bad for the stomach."

"And I had to buy polish for the harness, Seventy-nine cents."

"A few expenses," I tell her, "are to be expected."

"You should keep the accounts," she answers. "You should see how it all adds up!"

Sometimes I think too much business college is bad for a pretty girl, but the harm is done.

"I could cry," she says now. "You have bought a cat in a sack, papa, and all Pico Street knows it."

When we are finished, she clears the table, and I am glad for the rocking chair in the other room. Yet the ash falls from my cigarette with every noise in the kitchen.

"But we won't starve," Rosa is saying now. "I can always get a job in Pete Carillo's laundry. You and your merry-go-round!"

"That will not be necessary," I answer.

She comes now and sits beside me, her dish towel twisted in her hands. "I don't know what's the matter with me, papa."

I stroke her black hair. "We will not regret the merry-go-round," I say. "And one of these days a fine *caballero* will come riding a golden horse. Maybe tomorrow. You will see."

She shakes her head. "I do not want a *caballero*, papa. They are all a bunch of bums."

She is thinking of the boys in front of the Rio Grande Pool Hall maybe. She is not thinking of Sam Hondo, because he is a magnet still turned the wrong way to her.

Since the junk yard was sold, we have had no business to match the importance of Sam's garage.

I roll a good cigarette in brown paper. "We will not go broke with the merry-go-round," I say.

"But you cannot run it always at a loss," she answers. "And the organ is hanging by a thread."

It is too bad, I think to myself, *that a merry-go-round cannot be free to everybody.*

"I will see Sam Hondo in the morning," I say. "When the machinery is fixed, we will think of a way to get business."

But she is silent. She is thinking the thoughts of women and cats when there is rain on the roof.

"I'll shine the harness some more," she sighs finally, "but I don't know why."

Sam is under an automobile when I come in the garage and kick his foot.

He looks out to murder somebody, but his face spreads to a smile when he sees who it is. "Papa Gomez," he says, "I was just thinking about you."

I would rather his mind had been on Rosa.

"Because I have a merry-go-round to fix?" I ask.

"Sure." He wipes his wrench on his pants leg and holds out his cigarettes. "I hear there's to be a Christmas party," he says, "with pine trees and red wreaths. Free rides and oranges for everybody."

That is the way a thing grows. A stone at one end of Pico Street becomes a house at the other.

"I had not thought so far as that," I say carefully.

"It's a fine idea," he beams. "The kind of advertising that pays off. But you've got to have everything in good shape, Papa Gomez. You don't want a breakdown."

"All right, Sam," I answer, "come down and look it over. Make me a price."

He grins. "That means an itemized estimate for Rosa."

"Write is all down," I say. "She is particular."

"You're telling me." He whistles. "I'll add it twice and it'll still be wrong."

Because he is a boy you can talk to, I speak a little to relieve my mind. "You should hear her about the expenses already," I say. "You would think we will wind up in the poorhouse."

He wrinkles his forehead. "You got to watch the expenses, Papa Gomez; it's a fact. She's right there." He looks away to his office in the corner. "That's what I need—somebody to watch my expenses."

"Could be," I say, "you need a bookkeeper."

"Another expense," he frowns. "That is not the answer."

They are two of a kind, I think to myself.

"When you look at the merry-go-round," I say, "do not touch the organ or you will have to fight the man who runs it."

"I'll be there in an hour," he answers.

I do not go to the beach right away. I reason that when Sam comes to the merry-go-round and crawls into the machinery, Rosa will crawl in behind him to see what must be fixed. In such a dark hole there is room for more than curiosity.

It is lunchtime when I get to the merry-go-round.

Rosa should be waiting. There should be music. But everything is still. I see the three of them are sitting on the platform with their feet hanging over. They look at me, guilty as dogs with a dead chicken. They have been waiting.

"We broke the organ," Rosa says.

Sam's face is red as a chili pepper. "I broke it, you mean."

"No," Rosa says, "we did."

Potsie has eyes full of misery. "We thought to lift it and put tin cans under," he says.

"With water in," Rosa adds.

"To keep the termites out," Sam explains. "It was my idea."

"So there is no music?" I say gently. "How bad is the organ?"

"A box of sawdust," Potsie answers.

Sam is the first to give comfort. "The machinery is not so bad as you would think, Papa Gomez. I can fix it in good shape."

But Rosa looks to him without hope. "Of what good is that, after what happened?"

"It will not cost you a cent," he answers. "I will work tonight."

"We can afford to pay," she points out, "whatever is reasonable."

"There is yet two weeks of school vacation," Potsie observes. "The sooner she is running, the better."

"Fix it up," I say to Sam.

"But without music," Rosa insists, "who will pay the price to ride?"

"Exactly. Who will pay so much anyway?" I have thought of these prices all morning. It is a crime. I have bought this thing, in a way, for the little ones. *If I am to go bankrupt with bad luck*, I think, *I will do it right*. "My friends," I say, "we will let them ride free-for-nothing."

"Are you crazy, papa?" Rosa cries.

"That doesn't make sense, Papa Gomez," Sam agrees with her. "They should pay something."

"They can pay what they want to," I give in a little. "We will see. But first we must make it go."

Potsie is studying me like I am a bad piece of money. "Mr. Gomez," he says now, "you are going to go broke. That is bad. But I will help you. I will work for nothing."

Sam gets up now. "I'll be down after supper," he says. And then to Rosa, "Want to help tonight?"

"You mean see that you don't go to sleep," she answers. But she does not say it with sharpness.

Because they have broken a thing together, I think, *they are already closer.*

In the evening when supper is done, Rosa walks up and down the kitchen. Finally it comes out. "Maybe I should go down and see that he turns the lights out."

We are painting a cardboard sign which says: RIDE ALL YOU WANT; PAY WHAT YOU PLEASE.

"A man works better with a woman to watch him," I say carefully. "If he had a good supper, he will go to sleep."

"Exactly," she replies. "We must keep after him."

When she is gone, I put the sign to dry behind the stove. *A merry-go-round without music is like a parrot that cannot talk*, I think sadly. With Christmas but a week off, the party I have promised lies heavy on my heart.

In the morning it is raining, and I must ask Rosa to stop at Señora Cerrito's grocery store to speak for the oranges and pine trees.

"How was it last night with Sam?" I ask, as she pulls on her overshoes.

"When he works, he sees only the wrench in his hand," she says impatiently. "Such concentration!"

"It is done, then?"

"There are parts to make," she answers. "The machinery is all over the floor."

For four days it rains and Rosa will not let me from the house. Sam is working every night, and every day Potsie stands guard to keep the children from the pieces on the floor. Rosa is home only to get the meals, and I am a man in prison, counting the time that is left until the party.

On the day before Christmas, Rosa says the machinery is fixed, and goes off with the sign we have painted. It has stopped raining, and I am standing by the gate as Señora Gonzaga passes.

"We can hardly wait," she breathes to me. "You are very good, Señor Gomez. Pray God it will not rain to wet the snow."

"Snow?" I exclaim.

"But of course," she says. "We have heard the whole merry-go-round will be in snow."

"Mother of Mercy," I say. "In California there is snow only in the mountains."

"What's the difference," she says. "It will be cotton, but it will look like snow."

When Rosa returns, I mean to ask her about this snow, which will be another disappointment, but she is bursting at the seams with bad news, and Sam is with her.

"Potsie has disappeared!" she cries.

"He just walked off," Sam adds gloomily, "with a hundred kids wanting to ride. They are all over the place."

"Sam has to be at the garage," Rosa says. "I can't run the machinery by myself."

"What about the pine trees and the oranges?" I ask her.

"They're all set," Sam says. "The oranges are locked up in the box office."

"Potsie! That no-good Potsie!" Rosa moans.

I would speak about the snow, but it would only make matters worse. "These hundred little ones,'" I ask, "they want to ride even without music?"

Rosa pulls the berries from the mistletoe she is holding. "They don't know about the organ," she says. "They just saw the decorations."

"And the sign," Sam adds. "The news sure spread about that sign."

"Let it rest until tomorrow afternoon, then," I say. "If we are lucky, maybe it won't rain."

"Don't worry," Sam says to Rosa. "I'll run the machinery tomorrow. We'll have the party all right."

When he is gone, Rosa stares at the mess she has made with the mistletoe. It has been a week of worry.

She is a cat in the wind, I think, *with but one tongue to smooth her fur.*

"Sam is dead tired," she says finally. And then, in a voice I have not heard since she was ten years old, "Do you think he will remember to get me a present?"

"Fixing the merry-go-round is a present," I say gently.

From where it is hidden under her coat, she takes out a package. "Maybe I shouldn't have spent the money," she says, unwrapping a set of six small wrenches in oil paper. "I'll just cry if he forgets; I know I will."

As we sit at our Christmas breakfast of coffee and crackers, Rosa is a child again over the red purse I have given her from D'Este's Leather Shop.

"But you should not have had it made, papa," she cannot help saying, "not even for me."

On the table before me are many presents. A dozen brass rings from the hardware store. A copper oil can with a long spout. A new pair of police suspenders. And a ledger book with red corners, in which Rosa will keep the accounts of the merry-go-round.

"Actually, papa," she promises, "the merry-go-round is your best present." She squeezes my hand. "You will see!"

It is eleven-thirty when a car drives up in front with big signs on the sides. MERRY CHRISTMAS, the signs say: MEET SANTA CLAUS AT THE MERRY-GO-ROUND. A fat man in a red suit and white whiskers climbs out.

"Sam! Sam, you fool!" Rosa cries, and runs, laughing, from the porch.

When they are inside, I hold my breath, wondering if he has remembered. Rosa runs to the bedroom and returns with her package.

"Merry Christmas, Señor Santa Claus!" she says, her eyes shining.

Sam reaches into his hip pocket. "You thought I'd forget, didn't you?" he beams, and hands her a small package.

They peel off the papers, one faster than the other.

"A fountain pen and pencil!" Rosa cries. "Look, papa!"

"A set of jim-dandy wrenches!" Sam says. "See, Papa Gomez!"

If they knew what I was thinking, they would not understand. At their age, her mother would have had for me a yellow silk shirt, and I would have covered her eyes with kisses when I gave her flowers and a silver bracelet. But it is good, just the same, that he remembered.

"You should not have got the expensive set," Rosa is saying.

"You don't have to keep accounts with it," Sam replies; "you can keep a diary." He looks at me and winks. "And a small present for you, Papa Gomez."

From his other hip pocket he draws a package of the right size. It shakes well, and I set it carefully on the table. He is a good boy. With a nod, I thank him.

"It will come in handy," I say, "for the right occasion."

We drive to the beach in the automobile, with Sam putting his hand to the horn the length of Pico Street. Everybody looks to learn who has been married, and when the little ones see it is Santa Claus, they shout and begin running after us.

From where we park, we cannot see the merry-go-round until we have turned the corner.

"And now for the big surprise," Sam says.

He waves his arms, and as we look to it, the merry-go-round begins to move. But there is no sound.

Rosa grabs Sam by his red coat as he strides ahead. "Sam! It's going! There are kids on the horses!"

I rub my eyes. "Snow!" I cry. "It is impossible!"

Sam is like a small boy. "Stuffing from Descanso's Mattress Factory," he tells me, "that got wet in the fire. We must send it back tomorrow."

"See, papa!" Rosa cries. "We painted all the horses with new paint!"

"Automobile paint," Sam puts in. "The brightest colors in the book, all wholesale!"

"And the pictures at the top!" Rosa points. "Washed with soap and water!"

Sam is so excited he puts his arm around her. We are running now to see better. Then we hear the music. An old Italian in rags is standing inside. He has a black mustache, in his ears gold rings, a red handkerchief around his neck. He is grinding a small organ strapped to his shoulders.

"There he is," Sam laughs.

"He didn't run away!" Rosa cries. "Papa, look! It's Potsie!"

"He showed up at my place this morning," Sam whispers. "Said he sneaked off to get that old grinder fixed."

Potsie kicks out the stick and bows as we come to him.

"Señor! Señorita! How you likea takea ride?" He points to his hat on the floor. "How you likea these business, no?"

In the hat and on the floor are nickels and dimes and even quarters. He points to the sign: RIDE ALL YOU WANT: PAY WHAT YOU PLEASE. "If we had a monkey," he shouts, "we could make a million dollars!"

What can I say?

Already Pico Street is coming on a hundred legs. When Sam starts and stops the horses, there is a shower of money at Potsie and the hat. I climb to the high box where the bar is hung, and put in all the rings it will hold. Rosa is unpacking the crates, and when Sam is not at the machinery, he is Santa Claus with a bag full of oranges for the kids.

"What a day!" Celita Santee shouts to me. "Such a Christmas!" And I see with pleasure that her grandchildren are behind her.

Gringos have come to watch, and Sam is waving them to the empty horses. When every horse is full, Señor Velez is yet standing with three who suck oranges and cry to be on.

Rosa is beside herself, calling to Sam to stop oftener, so more can ride. I have seen that Potsie has on one shoe a sole with glue. When he steps on money, it disappears, and he picks it off his foot with a hand behind him. It is a way to keep the pile down, but not a thing to be forgotten.

In the crowd I have seen Señor La Paz leaning on his son. When Sam has stopped the machinery for a few minutes I see them talking. Señor La Paz is smiling, and steps forward with a small stick to measure a black horse from nose to tail. I look away so they will not know I have seen, but I tremble a little. In all of Santa Monica Cemetery there is not a stone horse. Mine will be the first.

Potsie is standing close to the merry-go-round and his grinder is fairly jumping as he turns the crank. The reason is not far to see. Rosa and Sam are on two horses, riding neck and neck, and on both faces a guilty look. They think they are too old for such foolishness. When Sam grabs a gold ring from the bar, he holds it up to me like it is the prize from a box of popcorn. When they come around again, he is leaning to Rosa.

Potsie has become a man on fire. He jumps on the platform and grinds his music in front of them. Everybody is looking now, and a great shout goes up when Sam puts the gold ring on Rosa's finger. Both look at me as they go around. Rosa holds up her hand.

I wave a blessing. But I am thinking of a little *caballero* with black eyes who will someday ride a golden horse on this merry-go-round. The garage business is a good business. There is no reason there should not be a fine organ as well.

MONEY IS NEVER A GIFT

"A great idea has come to me!" cries my uncle, Luis Gonzales. "Now we will be able to buy new school clothes for little Pedro!" He is full of joy.

My father, who is called José Gonzales, has heard many great ideas from my Uncle Luis. All bad. He is without approval. "Listen to him, Pedro!" he growls at me. "Luis is on the dream wagon again."

We are sitting on old boxes and oilcans in the city dump of Santa Monica. It is a clear, hot morning and the sun shines on the object in my Uncle Luis' hand as on a vessel of silver. He polishes it on his sleeve. He regards it with respect. It is a tin can.

"A thing I have noticed about people," he says, "is that they like to put money into tin cans. All that is required is a slot in the top."

I am picking the spokes of an old bicycle wheel, pretending it is a guitar. My father makes me be still. "Don't you want some new clothes?" he demands. "Don't you want to be rich?" Already he is making fun of my Uncle Luis' idea.

"There is such a can in the Acme butcher shop," my uncle informs him. "Once a week a man comes from the Community Chest to empty it."

"For that matter," says my father, "every store in California has a can for the governor in which is dropped pennies for taxes."

"There is also the Red Cross!" cries Uncle Luis. "There have been cans for the Italians and the Greeks and the Chinese. Does ths suggest nothing?"

"Nothing," my father replies sourly. "Nothing but trouble."

"It is necessary to have a can of the proper size," my uncle says quickly to make clear his idea. "If it is too big, people will be discouraged. If it is too small, they will overlook it."

"If one puts such a can to collect money for one's self, one will be arrested," my father says flatly.

Uncle Luis regards him with patience. "You do not understand," he explains. "We are a worthy cause. New school clothes for little Pedro are a necessary thing. A worthy cause is not put in jail."

My father grunts. "Throw the tin can away, Luis," he advises. "Free money is only for other people." After much looking this morning he has found a new rake handle to replace the one he has broken. He goes back now to whittling it to fit.

Uncle Luis holds the tin can in one hand and taps the top with his finger. "The lid must fit tightly," he says, "because there are people with too much curiosity. And the slot must be big enough for a fifty-cent piece."

"Why not a dollar?" my father asks gloomily.

"Because we are not greedy men," Uncle Luis replies.

When my eye lights on another can like the one he is cutting the slot in, I bring it to him. "With two cans," I suggest, "maybe we can all have new clothes."

My Uncle Luis nods approval. He studies both cans. "See, José, how the mind works at a good thing?"

My father's face has much tenderness as he looks at me. He rises. "The lawn I am cutting is far away," he says. "My feet will be tired before I get there." He takes the can from my hand and throws it into the dump. "Have nothing to do with these cans," he says. "And when you come home, see that you sweep out, and wash the dishes." With his rake over his shoulder, he climbs the embankment to the highway.

"Your father has been cutting the same lawn for three days, I think," Uncle Luis observes. "He is in a rut." He instructs me to find something that has the word "give" printed in big letters on it, and it is not long before I have found a miserable picture of a hungry little girl in a newspaper. There are big and little "gives" all around it. Uncle Luis finds some white paint in an old bucket. He cuts out a "give" with his knife and pastes it around the can. It is a very good job.

"There is nothing like a dump," he says, standing up. "Where there are six Americans in one place, one can live on what the other five throw away." He winks at me and pats my shoulder. "I am the sixth man," he says.

I roll the bicycle wheel I have found beside him, and we go behind a tile factory and through many alleys. We find a good oilstone, an electric-light socket and a bottle half full of white wine. "Never walk on the street," he advises me, as he finishes the wine, "if it is possible to walk in the alley. One can learn more from behind a house than in front of it."

We are but stepping from the alley into Pico Street when we hear a whistle out of nowhere, and Father Lomita in his black robe comes swinging down upon us. His whistle is known to all. He is a priest who can see through nine pairs of pants.

My Uncle Luis pushes the can into his coat, but not, I think, before the swift eyes of the padre have seen it. He bids us good morning.

"A beautiful day," my Uncle Luis replies, and stands with his hat in his hand.

Father Lomita reminds us that this is Saturday, the day of Our Lady of Mount Carmel, and that tomorrow is the sixth Sunday after Pentecost. "You will not forget to be on time in the morning," he says, smiling down on me, and I think, too, he is studying where I have got the bicycle wheel. Because I am an altar boy, Father Lomita takes a great interest in me. It has been a sad worry to him that my mamma ran off to Salinas with a lettucepicker from the Imperial Valley.

"And how is your papa José?" he asks.

"He is cutting a lawn today," I reply. "He is thinking of getting me some new school clothes."

Father Lomita is happy to hear this. "Have you ever thought about cutting lawns, too, Luis?" he asks.

"Never," my uncle replies.

"It is an idea," Father Lomita suggests.

"That is true," Uncle Luis agrees. "I had not looked at it in just that way before."

His bus is coming and Father Lomita must run, but not before he has reminded me again that tomorrow is Sunday.

"It is a fine day for feeling good!" Uncle Luis shouts to Señor Santee at the poultry store as we pass. And at Manuel Velez's barbership he makes Manuel a small gift of the oilstone. Because my Uncle Luis has the idea of the tin can, he is rich in his mind and of a good humor.

"Rest awhile," says Manuel, "and little Pedro can sweep out the shop." He is a man to find jobs for other people.

But when he reaches for the broom, Uncle Luis waves it aside. "I have a little business at the Caliente Café," he says. "I have a desire to see my dear friend Carmelita."

This is the first I have heard of where we are going. For a long time Carmelita Smith made hamburgers at a stand on the beach, but now she is behind the cash register at the Caliente Café.

"I hear Mike Lopez has asked you to play the guitar at the Caliente," Manuel observes. "That would be a warm spot on cold nights."

"My guitar is in the hock shop," Uncle Luis explains. "I loaned Carmelita ten dollars to buy Mexican clothes for her new job. She has not paid back yet, so there is no guitar."

"A misfortune," breathes Manuel. "It seems one cannot have everything." He puts the barber comb through his own hair. "At least she is trying to get you a job where she can watch you."

"She is a woman who is liking music," Uncle Luis replies.

There is a big sign over the Caliente Café which says: TACOS—TORTILLAS—ENCHILADAS—TAMALES—LUNCHES—DINNERS—MEXICAN MUSIC. Under the porch are hung strings of gourds and chili peppers. I do not believe the words, NEW MANAGEMENT, because they are printed on an old card which is always put up when business is bad. Señor Lopez, who runs the Caliente Café, thinks all gringos are *stupidos*. The MEXICAN MUSIC is a lie. There has not been any music since he was cut in the chest by a girl marimba player he had forgotten to pay. Mike Lopez is a sour man, and my Uncle Luis says someday he will poison the gringos with bad grub and be sent to prison.

"But it is still the best place to put our tin can," he observes to me. "It is only the gringos who have money."

It is lunchtime when we walk into the shade of the porch. A few women who look like schoolteachers are at the tables picking wax drip from the candle bottles. Señor Mike Lopez, with a red sash around his big stomach, is pretending to them that he does not speak English.

Carmelita Smith, in her new clothes, is sitting on a high stool behind the cash register. She has gold earrings and a dark skin. It is said that she is part gypsy and has the blood of the *gitanos* in her veins. It is said that she carries a small knife in the top of her stocking and can make coins disappear while you are looking at them. She is what my Uncle Luis calls a quick cat, and they have known each other a long time. When he winks at her, she returns him a big smile. He leans his elbow on the counter and takes a toothpick from the white saucer.

"How is business?" he inquires when he has chewed the toothpick.

"A big crowd last night," she answers, "but I can't pay you back yet."

"It is nothing," he answers. Carmelita gives him a quick look, but my Uncle Luis studies the ceiling. "It is a fine thing that Lopez permits you to keep the mistakes in making change."

"It is the only way," she replies proudly. "I have never worked for wages in my life."

"A thing I have admired in you," Uncle Luis admits.

Señor Lopez has opened the tamales for the happy ladies and comes to us now, wiping his hands on the back of his pants. "Well, Luis," he demands through his black mustache, "have you found your guitar?"

My uncle shrugs. "I was very drunk when I lost it. It could be anywhere."

Señor Lopez shows his teeth. "For myself, I hate music," he says, "but it helps to loosen up the gringos. Maybe if you look in the hock shop your guitar will turn up."

"It is possible," my uncle replies.

"I have offered to give you half of the tips you get." Señor Lopez rubs his hands. "It is a fair deal."

"Perhaps," yawns my Uncle Luis.

"My uncle is the best guitar player on all Pico Street," I put in to help matters.

"So!" Señor Lopez cries, and lifts me by the hair. "Little Pedro is hoping to pass the sombrero!"

"Put him down." Uncle Luis regards Señor Lopez with a sleepy eye. "Perhaps we can do business." He draws from his pocket the tin can with the slot in the top and sets it beside the cash register. He explains how the can is to be used. "I will play my guitar in your lousy joint every night on two conditions." He counts them off on his fingers. "First, you will loan me ten dollars to recover my guitar."

"Agreed," nods Señor Lopez. He is studying the tin can like a man who has found a gold nugget. He peels off the money from a roll in his pocket. "Provided that you do not take the guitar out of my café until the sawbuck is paid back," he adds.

"Agreed," my uncle says. "And second" — he touches the tin can — "you are to keep your hands off this can."

Señor Lopez is slow to speak, and I see he is turning many things over in his mind. But he figures if he wants my uncle to play music, he had better say yes. "Agreed," he says, and shows his big teeth in a smile like he gives to the gringos. "A worthy cause is a worthy cause."

"Live and let live," my uncle replies, and folds the ten dollars he had got into a small square.

Carmelita Smith has been listening with very dark eyes, and she picks up the can and studies it. She regards my Uncle Luis with much respect. "If I am asked about this can," she observes, "it will be worth something to make the right answer."

"That is true," my Uncle Luis nods. "But there is a small matter between us which may now be forgotten." He means the ten dollars, but Señor Lopez does not know this, and there is a big suspicion in his face.

"I will say the can is for our people," Carmelita suggests, now that she and my uncle understand each other better. In her voice there is a deep sadness. "I will say the poor we have with us always."

Señor Lopez has reached to a hook for his coat. He goes to the ladies at the table to explain that he is called away suddenly to burn a candle in the church. He announces to Uncle Luis, "We will go now and get the guitar together." It is plain he does not trust my uncle with the ten dollars.

"I will take care of your can, Luis," Carmelita promises.

"Pedro," my uncle instructs me, "it will improve your arithmetic if you stay here with Carmelita and count any coins which are given to a worthy cause."

When they move into the shadow of the porch, Carmelita looks after them with a slow smile in her black eyes. She peels the paper from a stick of gum and tells me to shut my eyes and open my mouth. When I look again, she is laughing, and begins to pull packages of cigarettes and bars of candy from behind my ears. When Carmelita laughs she is very beautiful. It is hard to believe that she has a knife with a pearl handle and seven rubies in the top of her stocking.

When she has taken care of the ladies at the table, and they are standing at the desk to pay, they observe the can and read that it says to "give."

"They are a proud people," one of the ladies whispers. "They try to take care of one another." She drops a nickel in the slot. The others put in money too.

"*Gracias!*" breathes Carmelita.

"Is there much unemployment among you?" the lady who has put in the first nickel asks.

"Almost everybody has it," Carmelita sighs. "It is an affliction of my people." She has been counting out their change and the ladies are dividing what they have paid among themselves. Carmelita discovers she has given them too much, or maybe they have given her too little. Soon everybody is confused, and Carmelita is in tears. "I do no understand these money too much," she says, "because I am only a poor girl and have not learned business."

After they are gone, she jingles a few coins and slips them into a bag which she hides in the big pocket of her dress. Her eyes are dancing. "My darling," she asks, "how would you like a fat enchilada?"

My mouth is watering, for I have not eaten since coffee and one tortilla for breakfast.

"If you can make it disappear before Mike Lopez returns, I will give you one."

I promise. And When Señor Lopez and Uncle Luis walk in the door, I am licking my chops. Señor Lopez carries the guitar, tied up in a sack. "You must be here before six o'clock tonight," he says to Uncle Luis. "And it would be a good idea if you tried to sing when you play."

He could not have insulted my uncle better. It is my father, José, who has the voice. Uncle Luis sings like a frog, but he keeps his mouth tight as he picks up the can and shakes it with a gentle motion. The coins make a sweet sound.

"How many, Pedro?" he asks.

"Five," I reply quickly.

"If you touch this can or scratch my guitar," he promises Señor Lopez, "I will give you a bad time." He winks at Carmelita and takes me by the shoulder. We pass through the shade under the porch and into the street.

The afternoon has turned hot, and we are both very sorry for my papa José. If he is smelling the wind from the sea over his hot lawn he is very unhappy. "He is working hard today," my uncle sighs. "Since he is fond of halibut, it is only right that we should go to the pier and catch one."

When we return home, my father is already there. He has spread out a handful of cigarette butts from the tobacco can and is hunting for the brand he likes. He sits in his bare feet, resting, and on the table is a big chocolate cake.

"Coming home, I saw it in the window," he says proudly. "I had just enough money to buy it."

"You have done a beautiful thing," my Uncle Luis praises him. "Besides, we are going to be rich anyway." While we clean our fish, he tells my father about the tin can and what is already in it. He speaks of the agreement with Señor Lopez, and of Carmelita, who is protecting the can.

"I do not like the whole thing," my father says with much worry. "This money is a bad thing, and there will be a fight over it before you are through."

Uncle Luis shrugs. "Lopez is a dog," he observes. "He suggested that I sing when I play the guitar. He knows I cannot sing."

My father is very quiet. But when we have fried the halibut and eaten it, and there is no more chocolate cake, he speaks what is on his mind. "I will go with you tonight," he declares.

While Uncle Luis protests that there will be no trouble, my father instructs me to wash my face and clean up, so I will not be a disgrace to the family.

There is already a small crowd of gringos at the Caliente Café when we arrive. Señor Lopez has put a sign in the window announcing Luis Gonzalez and his famous guitar. Since my uncle is well known for his guitar on Pico Street, many of our friends are already gathered on the warm benches in the dark of the porch. When they see that my father has come to sing, they cry to be sure and play Adiós! Mariquita Linda! Mañanitas, and many other songs.

The tin can is still beside the change mat on the desk, and Uncle Luis gives Carmelita a big smile. Señor Lopez produces the guitar, and inquires if Uncle Luis has brought his voice, meaning my father.

"I do not expect you to pay me for singing," my father informs him. He has been inspecting the tin can. "It is already pretty heavy," he whispers to me, and with a sad face sets it down again, as if it is a thing of evil which would be nice to keep.

Señor Lopez is clapping his hands and announces to the gringos in a big voice that the Gonzalez brothers, Luis and José, have consented to present the true music of Mexico, which cannot be found anywhere in Southern California but at the Caliente Café.

Uncle Luis strikes the chords and runs the melody of La Canción Mixteca. My father begins in a high, sweet tenor voice to sing. When my father sings, it is always with great feeling, and the words that he is far from the soil where he was born, and a great homesickness invades his thoughts, bring tears to the eyes of all who listen. "Oh, land of the sun!" he sings, "I sigh to see you! For I live without light, without love!" The chords from the guitar are like a woman crying in an empty church.

As they walk among the tables, I see that Carmelita Smith is staring down at the many rings on her fingers. When she lifts her eyes to Uncle Luis, it is with much affection. It comes to me that Carmelita will never steal my uncle's money from the can. But she would steal my Uncle Luis if he was not a man who nails himself down.

When they are treated to wine by the gringos, I see that Uncle Luis refuses to take money. "There is a tin can on the desk as you pay," he says. "There are those who will be grateful."

He has found a way to fox Señor Lopez out of his half of the tips. It has been agreed that Lopez will not touch the can. As the gringos go out and others come in, much money is dropped into the slot. Carmelita sees that none forget. I am a sure shot to have new school clothes now.

But Señor Lopez stands watching the can like a lizard with a fly. Because he does not look unhappy, I think he has figured out something too. He is too puffed up.

"See," my Uncle Luis whispers to me when I am standing beside him. "A coin is a small thing. But it is not a small thing to make people happy. Observe the look on the face. It is the same look which comes in a church . . . and see what a saving of equipment."

"Do you remember Adiós! Mariquita Linda?" my father asks of me.

It is an *amorcita* to which he has taught me the words, but I am struck with fright.

"You will sing with us this time," he says gently. "It is a beautiful song and good for people's hearts."

My Uncle Luis runs the chords and the melody. My father squeezes my arm and we begin, "*I am going away, because now you do not love me as I love you. Adios! Mariquita chula!*" I shut my eyes to everything and hear only the guitar and my father. The harmony is full of sweetness, and in my father's voice is the high quaver of sorrow. "*I am giving to you my very last good-by! Adiós! Mariquita linda!*" When it is over, there is a great shouting of approval from under the porch, and the gringos clap their hands and beat the glasses with forks and spoons.

But my heart jumps to my teeth when I see Father Lomita has come in and is sitting with another priest on the bench by the door.

"That is all," my father says. "You will go now and sit by the desk with Carmelita."

"Keep your eye on the tin can," Uncle Luis says. "You will see how your song will help to fill it."

"By the door," I manage to whisper. "There is Father Lomita."

My Uncle Luis looks, and his fingers make a nervous drumming on the belly of the guitar. "We are doing no sin," he says. But just the same he looks guilty.

"If he should inquire about that tin can," my father groans, "I will be cutting the church grass free for a year."

"He cannot know we have anything to do with it," Uncle Luis answers. "He will think the can belongs to Lopez."

"He saw it in your hand this morning," I remind him, "before you stuck it under your coat."

"*Perdición!* It is possible!" Uncle Luis' fingers jump up and down the neck of the guitar in light chords of many keys. "Tell Carmelita to hide the can," he instructs me. "Quick, before the padre sees it!"

My father whispers that they had best do another song and keep Father Lomita's mind on the music.

I am approaching the desk when I find Señor Lopez moving before me with a towel over his arm. He tells Carmelita he is going to read the cash register. I almost cry out, for I have seen that he is hiding another tin can under the towel.

"You can take a minute to rest," he says to her. "I will watch the desk."

Carmelita does not know about the tin can under the towel. She thinks maybe he is being nice for a change, and that Uncle Luis will watch him anyway. She goes quickly.

Señor Lopez has put down his towel on the counter and it covers the tin can from sight. It comes to me that the can he has been carrying is also under the towel, and that he is going to pick up the full one and leave the empty one.

It is true. He lifts the towel, and stands smiling like a man who has had a chicken lay an egg in his hand. Only a sharp eye would see that the "give" he has pasted on the new can is not exactly the same.

My uncle is far down the room, and Carmelita is slow to return. In a minute he will be gone with the money. What is worse, Father Lomita will still think that the empty can on the counter belongs to my Uncle Luis, and that he is shaving things too close again for the good of his soul. Since he has often said that he doubts my Uncle Luis' influence on me is for the best, I must do something quick.

I walk to the desk like I am doing nothing. Señor Lopez looks over my head. I remember some things I have seen Carmelita do, and with my elbow I knock off a few candy bars from the desk. Señor Lopez is quick to see what has fallen to the floor. In the second his eyes are turned, I grab the can from the desk and put it in my shirt. The next minute I am helping him pick up the candy, and he is twisting my ear for a little *stupido*. I bite his hand, and when we stand up again we are grinning into each other's faces so nobody will catch on.

Carmelita has come back to the cash register and has angry eyes. She sees that the can is missing. She is fixing the comb in her hair and signaling with a finger behind her head to Uncle Luis. Señor Lopez is sliding his big stomach around the desk and is holding the wad of towel in his hand like it is something he is going to throw away. I am trying to make Carmelita understand that the can with the money is inside the towel.

A hand is laid on my shoulder. It is not pressed hard, but it holds me to the floor. It is a very firm hand. When I am able to look up, it is into the stern face of Father Lomita.

"Isn't there something you should put back?" he asks.

"Put what back?" cries Señor Lopez with a guilty face.

But Father Lomita thinks he has the right rabbit by the ear already, and does not know a thief when he sees one.

"It is nothing," he says to Señor Lopez. "I was only speaking to little Pedro."

Suddenly Carmelita's arms are around me. "What are they doing to you, my poor *niño*?" she cries in anger. "What are they saying you have done?" I am smothered against her warm breast, and in a twinkling her fingers are inside my shirt and the cold can is gone from against my skin. She is putting her handkerchief to my eyes as if I have been crying, and is telling Father Lomita he is a good man, indeed, to accuse a child of stealing.

Father Lomita is very sober and his eyes are sad. "There was a can for money on the counter," he says. "Sometimes we are all tempted beyond our strength. It is nothing that will not be forgiven."

My Uncle Luis and my father are there now, and begin to speak at once. "It is my tin can!" Uncle Luis confesses to help me. "He was only trying to hide it so you would not see it."

"Come here!" my father commands me. "Stand straight!" He motions Carmelita away. "Search him!" he demands of Father Lomita.

I think that my father has seen Carmelita take the can and he is being rough with me because I have nothing to lose.

But Father Lomita shakes his head. "If Pedro says he does not have it, that is enough."

"It is not enough!" my father answers, and shakes me from head to foot. when no can falls out, he beams on Father Lomita as if he has done a miracle.

My uncle has been searching the eyes of Carmelita, and they have come to an answer. He looks upon us all with much suspicion. "The can is gone," he announces. "There was much money in it. Somebody has it!"

I see that Señor Lopez has his eyes turned to the ceiling and is holding the wad of towel behind him. The room is very still. The gringos are staring at us from the tables, and Father Lomita's face is very white. He feels he has done a thing which was unjust.

"Father Lomita!" I burst out. "It is true that you saw me take the can! But it was only to hide it."

Suddenly Carmelita lets out a scornful laugh. She has slipped behind Señor Lopez and now rips the towel from his hand. "Here is the guilty one!" she cries, and the tin can falls to the floor with a great tinkling. She kicks it to Father Lomita's feet.

Señor Lopez stands like a man who has had a bucket emptied upon his head. The can is there, and he cannot argue. Since he is discovered before all, a great shame covers him, and he has nothing to say.

"Robber!" cries my Uncle Luis. "Dog of a thief!"

My father is standing very stiff. He is thinking how he can keep us out of trouble. With a great sigh he picks up the can and puts it into Father Lomita's hands. "We had an idea with this can," he says slowly, "to take gifts. We have not said so much, but it was in our mind to give the money to a worthy cause."

Father Lomita holds the can, turning it over in his hand for a long time. "Thank you, José," he says at last. "There are many people in the world who have less even than we do here."

"*Gracias*," whispers my father, and he puts his arm softly around my shoulders.

He has given the padre my new clothes.

A great weight has fallen from my Uncle Luis when he sees what my father has done. He leans now beside Carmelita with his guitar under his arm. "There is always somebody else worse off," he says happily.

Señor Lopez stands like a dog who has been chased from a yard. But Father Lomita speaks kindly to him. "When you feel like it, come and talk to me."

"I will come," Señor Lopez promises. "*Gracias*, padre. I will come."

"Perhaps all of you had better come sometime soon," Father Lomita suggests. When he has patted my head and said everything is for the best, he and the other priest bid us good night.

At once Carmelita Smith and Uncle Luis and my father face Señor Lopez and announce that this is the end.

Carmelita declares it is all over with her behind the cash register, and Uncle Luis is ready to walk out with his guitar.

"You would let a child be blamed for stealing an empty can!" Carmelita accuses him. "You are a great pig!"

"I am a pig then," he apologizes. Señor Lopez has a very long face, but he is working overtime in his head. "Which of you has the other can?" he demands.

Carmelita draws it from her dress and places it upon the desk. "There are many good causes!" she declares.

My Uncle Luis runs a few chords on the guitar. "Is it true that I owe a pig ten dollars?" he inquires of Señor Lopez.

There is a long meeting of eyes. "It is not true," Señor Lopez answers. "You have mistaken me for somebody else."

"Live and let live," says my Uncle Luis.

The gringos, who do not understand what has happened, are crying for more songs. My father stands undecided. He is a man who likes to sing. He looks to the can on the desk and is perhaps considering the fine gift we have been able to make to Father Lomita. There is still the matter of my school clothes.

Señor Lopez scoops up a few candy bars from the desk and presses them into my hands. "When we are better friends," he says, "you will see I am not the worst pig in the world."

Uncle Luis nods to my father. "You see," he observes, "there is more than one kind of riches in a tin can."

Carmelita leans her brown elbows on the desk and smiles into my Uncle Luis' eyes. "A good wind is blowing tonight, amigo," she says softly.

"A night for music," my uncle agrees.

Señor Lopez lifts his hand to the gringos for silence. Uncle Luis runs his fingers among the soft, light chords. The candy is sweet in my mouth, and tomorrow I will be the best altar boy in all California. Soon I will have new clothes for school. Someday I will have a guitar of my own, like Uncle Luis, and a voice to put tears in people's hearts, like my father.

A TRUCK FOR THE BOSS

The boss has fired me. He slaps my shoulder. "Diego," he says, "if I had one more truck, I could keep you on." He is a sad man. He looks at the whole Pacific Ocean and shakes his head.

I, too, am sad. This morning another truck fell into the sea. My job went with it. My job was an easy one. It is a great loss to me. It is not every day one can come by a job so pleasant as pointing a finger to where a rock should be put.

We are building a sea wall at Redondo Beach to keep the waves out. We stand watching the few trucks that are hauling boulders from the rock quarry. They have here a silly idea to outsmart the ocean. This job could have lasted as long as there is an ocean.

"Boss," I ask, "if I can line up another truck for you, do I get my job back?"

"This work is murder on trucks," he says. "We can't even rent another one." He looks me over with his sad eyes. "What makes you think you can get one?"

The reason is, of course, that I am Diego Cordoniz. But this is not a thing to speak aloud. "I have connections," I say. "Do I get my job back?"

"I'd give my shirt for another truck," he groans.

This is a promise. Plainly, I have now only to get a truck. I hitch up my pants and start for the highway. "See you *mañana*, boss!" I promise.

His laugh is like an echo from a tunnel. It means that he expects never to see me again. He does not understand that I will go to great lengths to keep a job with which I am *simpático*. He does not appreciate my feeling for dumping rocks into the sea.

The one to help me is my lucky cousin, Juan Cordoniz, of Sepulveda Boulevard. But I have not seen him for more than a year. Not since his wedding to the rich Chiquita Delgadillo. Until this morning, the rumor that he has bought a new truck was of no importance to me. Now I am hoping that this truck is a big one, and that my cousin has forgotten how drunk I was at his wedding. Also, I am thinking how to renew his friendship in a gentle way.

My throat is very dry by the time I reach Pico Street in West Los Angeles. There are yet a few miles between me and my cousin's farm. Suddenly, while I am thinking where to get a glass of wine, I see a big green truck in front of the poultry store. Printed on the side in red letters is the name, JUAN CORDONIZ. I rub my hands and approach.

I have put only a foot on the hub of the wheel, thinking to roll a cigarette, when my cousin appears beside me as if he had sprung from the concrete.

"So! Diego Cordoniz!" he says without relish.

"It has been a long time," I smile.

"Not since the wedding," he reminds me. "You disgraced us all before the Delgadillos."

I see he has not forgotten the affair of the Delgadillos' front door, which I took off the hinges, so it would not have to be opened and shut. A good idea at the time.

"Your wife, Chiquita?" I inquire politely. "She is well?"

"Never better," he scowls. "I suppose you are on your way someplace."

"No," I begin. I see he wishes me on the other side of the Tehachapi Mountains, but this is to be expected. "I am in town on business," I continue. "Come, have a glass of wine with me."

"No, thanks!" he says. He has wet a finger and is wiping a bug speck from the green paint. There is an impatience about him which I do not remember.

"This is a fine truck," I say pleasantly.

"A fine responsibility," he grumbles.

I examine it with much admiration. "It is like new. You have not used it at all."

"I've had it ten months," he informs me. "I take good care of it."

It occurs to me that getting his truck to the sea wall will not be an easy matter. Never have I seen a man more careful of a thing.

"Why have a truck and not use it?" I ask. "You must be too rich to work."

"Rich?" he cries, putting his nose close. "I'm poorer than I ever was! This morning I brought in eggs. Where does the money go? I'll show you!" He runs into the poultry store and returns with a sack on each shoulder. "For chicken feed!" he groans.

Caramba! you would think he could not afford to feed his miserable chickens! I feel a perversity rising in me. It is well known that on the wedding day rich Señor Delgadillo gave to his daughter one thousand dollars in cold cash. How can a man feel so poor with such riches? Does he not have a farm of an entire acre of black dirt on the boulevard? *If he cannot feed his chickens*, I think to myself, *I will be happy to help him eat them.* The matter of the truck is getting nowhere. I see he must be approached carefully.

"You are going home now?" I ask.

"Yes," he says. "Today is irrigation. More money poured in the ground."

"I will ride with you," I say. "I would like to pay my respects to Chiquita." To this I do not see how he can object. On the way I must make an opportunity to talk business.

"I have no insurance for medical payments," he declares. "I do not like to ride people."

"Medical payments?"

"There are many accidents," he explains; "people are hurt."

He should see the accidents at the sea wall! I laugh in his face. "I am prepared to die any time," I say as I crawl into the truck. *What has come over him?* I wonder. *A year ago he was like a feather on the wind.* "I suppose you have a good thing in this trucking business," I begin, when we are started.

"I do not talk when I drive," he answers. "One must keep his mind on the road."

This to me, who have sat a hundred times with sleeping drivers coming down the curves from the rock quarry. A good driver wakes up only at stop lights. I myself have driven a truck occasionally. It is nothing.

His head is turning in all directions to see that we will not be hit. There is sweat on his face. Plainly, he is afraid. I look to the dashboard. In this truck of my cousin there is not only one medal of Saint Christopher but four of them. This is over-doing it.

After a few miles we swing from the highway into a little road. Chickens fly up from the dust on all sides as we roll to the barn. It is not a barn to speak of. It is old and without paint. The house is small, and the porch is without a roof. A washing is blowing on the line between two eucalyptus trees.

Already Chiquita is running to us through the dust. She is barefooted, and the wet suds fly from her fingers. By the saints, she is beautiful!

"Cousin Diego!" she cries, wiping her hands on her apron. "How nice to see you again!" When she has greeted me, she hugs my cousin as if he had just come home from a year at sea.

Ay! I think, *This sour relative of mine is crazy.* Even now, he stands wrapped in a cloud of worry.

"You should have waited for me to help with the washing," he scolds her. "I told you I would do my pants and the heavy things."

I am thunderstruck that a Cordoniz should even think of such a thing. "He is joking," I smile. "Perhaps you do not get the dirt out of things."

My cousin turns angry. "What she needs is a washing machine, like other women," he says. "But there is no money — no money for anything."

"I can tell you how to make money," I begin.

But suddenly he has seen the water spreading from a ditch in the field. "I must get out there!" he cries. "Where is my irrigation shovel?"

"Can't it wait a little while?" Chiquita says. "There is no place for the water to go but in the ground."

"I must get to work," he says, "but first I must put the truck in the shade."

I'll be a Mission Indian! He runs that truck into the barn and puts a big canvas over it like a nightgown.

"The chickens mess it up," Chiquita informs me. "I'll swear, he thinks more of that truck than he does of me." She does not say this happily, I observe.

If she is jealous of this truck, I think to myself, *perhaps she will help me*.

"When Juan comes in, we must have a glass of wine," she is saying. "I have thought many times how you enjoyed the wine at our wedding." She laughs a little as she remembers.

She is a woman of understanding!

"What is the matter with my cousin?" I ask quickly. "He has become a heavy man. A worrier."

"It's the truck," she says. "It's all so silly."

She is bending to work the cork from a bottle when my cousin rushes in.

"None for me," he says. "I only want my rubber boots."

"Just a little," she begs, "in honor of Cousin Diego."

Dog of a dog! Since when does a Cordoniz not have time to take wine? She even puts the glass in his hand. When he drinks, it is as if he is being made to spend a dollar.

"What brings you to West Los Angeles?" Chiquita asks of me.

This is my chance. "Business," I begin. "I am working on the Redondo sea wall. The boss needs some more trucks. I thought there was a possibility —"

My cousin appears suddenly to have swallowed a tarantula from his wineglass. "If you are thinking of my truck" — he glares at me — "you are wasting your time."

"Such a thing never entered my mind." I protest. "But now that you mention it—"

"Nothing could ruin a truck quicker," he says. "I have heard all about that sea wall."

"Yes," I say quickly, "but perhaps you do not know all the angles to it. There is a thing or two that—"

"You are wasting your breath," he cuts me off. "And while I stand here I am wasting good water." He is a driven man for sure. "Come out in the field," he says, banging the screen door; "I'll put you to work."

"Do not feel you must entertain me," I say to Chiquita when he is gone.

"You can watch me wash," she smiles.

"And you can tell me what is eating on my cousin."

"I do not think I should talk about it," she says.

"Then I will tell you my own troubles," I say sadly. "I need another truck for the boss at the sea wall. If I cannot rustle up another truck, I am out of a job. Juan could help me and make a lot of money for himself as well."

The splashing stops. "I wish he would," she sighs, "but nothing could be more impossible."

"You can speak freely to me," I encourage her. "What makes him so screwy about this truck of his?"

"He thinks it doesn't belong to him, that's all."

"Not his?" I ask in alarm.

"No. You see, when we were married my father gave me a sum of money—a thousand dollars."

"So I have heard."

"We put it as a down payment on the truck."

"Yes?"

"Now Juan thinks the truck belongs more to me than to him. That's why he's so careful of it."

"But it's a good investment!" I exclaim with relief. "A fine thing."

"You don't understand," she sighs. "He thought I should have spent the money on myself—for a washing machine, a radio, some good clothes."

"He's nuts!" I say. "With such a truck, he can make enough money for all these things."

"Of course," she agrees. "But he will not use it until it is paid for. He will haul nothing heavy to hurt it. He is afraid even to drive it, for fear something will happen to it."

"*Perdón!*" I despair. "My cousin has become a bookkeeper — even with his wife!"

"He is trying to make the farm pay for everything," she goes on. "He wishes he could return to me my part of the investment, so I can have the things for the house." She throws up her hands. "What can you do with a man like that?"

"If I did not need that truck myself," I say honestly, "I would tell you to sell it."

"He loves that thing!" she cries. "He would never part with it!"

"We must change his mind," I say firmly. "We must do something quick. I must have this truck by tomorrow."

"If I were you," she answers, "I'd look someplace else for a truck."

"But there is no place else to look!"

If I were not myself, Diego Cordoniz, I think I would give up. I would forget about my true place at the sea wall. But it is not in my character to do this. When Chiquita bends over the tub again, I head for the field where my cousin is working. Until I can get a toe hold in his mind, I will speak only of the smallest things.

"Fine cabbages," I observe. "You have a nice place here."

"Nice mortgage, you mean!" My cousin leans on his shovel. "Between the bank and the finance company, I am about to give up."

"How deep are they into you?" I ask. I sound like the proprietor of a pawnshop I know in San Pedro. A man of business.

Perhaps my cousin suspects I have saved a little money from working. Perhaps I am only somebody to talk to. A sickly laugh comes out of him. "Two thousand, three hundred and sixty-four dollars," he groans, "and forty-one cents."

"*Una fortuna!*" I exclaim with admiration. But I am wondering if he is counting Chiquita's thousand in this figure. "How much to the bank?" I inquire.

"Four hundred."

"And to the finance company?"

"Nine sixty-four, forty-one."

We stand looking at each other like two lizards in the sun. He knows I can add. "We are yet a thousand short," I observe.

The look he throws me is like a fish spear. A redness creeps into his ears.

"That is owing to another party," he says as if he is ashamed. "I do not wish to speak about it."

I would feel sorry for my dumb cousin if I did not want his truck so much. I begin to argue. "Your troubles would be over if you took a hauling contract on the sea wall."

"I am taking no contracts," he says angrily, "until I have the pink slip on my truck."

"This other party you speak of," I begin carefully — "this other party has an interest in the truck?"

"That is a possibility," he says suspiciously.

Because I do not want him to know that Chiquita has let the cat out of the bag to me, I try to look innocent. But I must make progress. "If this other party you speak of is paid off," I say in a general way, "would it make a difference about the truck?"

A faint light comes in his eyes. Perhaps he thinks I am carrying a thousand dollars in my pocket. "Sure," he says, "it would make a big difference!"

I am not without understanding of his problem. It is often not so much the debt as to whom it is owed. Money borrowed within the family is as full of spines as a cactus. Because I can see a little daylight in this matter of the truck, I am struck full of generosity.

"I will get you this thousand dollars!" I promise him, with a slap on the back. "Such a sum is nothing to Diego Cordoniz. We will pay off this party you speak of and start a small company for ourselves. We will take a contract for hauling boulders at the sea wall. We will have work as long as there is an ocean."

"You're crazy," he says, sticking his shovel in the water. "You don't know what a thousand dollars looks like!"

"Allright!" I cry. "But is it a deal?"

"Sure, it's a deal," he says, as if he is calming a lunatic. "Go right ahead!"

"You will never regret it!" I say with much confidence. Under my ribs there is a hollow feeling which was not there before. But I walk away as if I am about to write out the check.

I have been in many tight places. Often a stick or a string is enough to save the day. A miserable sum of money should not be so hard to get if one but puts his mind to it. Even a thousand dollars. Already I am nearer to the truck. I have got the truck for the boss, so to speak, if I can locate a thousand dollars to clear my cousin with his wife. I look for the answer.

There is a rabbit hutch with a few white animals which suggest nothing. A pen without a pig. A patch of garden inside a fence of slats from orange crates.

I drift to the barn and sit on the tongue of a plow. I roll a cigarette. The truck is like a corpse under the white canvas. The miserable chickens pick at my shoestrings. In my trouble I have become very hungry.

Before it is suppertime I help Chiquita kill one of these stupid birds. I chop the parsley and green onions for putting on the chicken enchiladas. I tell her of my talk with Juan, and we discuss how a person might come by a thousand dollars. We end up exactly where we started. "Juan has his ideas," she sighs. "It will take more than talk to change him." Already I see she feels bad for having told me what was eating on my cousin. She is a good wife.

"It is a lucky thing," my cousin remarks when we are at the table, "that there are still some white Leghorns left."

This, I consider, is meant to make the enchiladas stick in my throat.

We do not speak more about the truck. Yet I have no intention of leaving this place without it. Because the evening is cool, we sit by the stove and smell the good smoke of eucalyptus wood. I relate a few stories I have picked up. When we are yawning in one another's faces, and I am still there, it is obvious I will spend the night.

"Chiquita will find you an extra blanket," my cousin says finally. "This floor in here is not too hard." When she has gone out, he gives me a dirty look. "I see you have not raised the money yet. Perhaps it will come to you in a dream."

"A little time is required," I say. "I must make certain connections."

What these connections will be I have no idea. I listen to the ashes settle in the stove. I am thinking of the boss and his empty laugh. My unhappy cousin is convinced I am loco. Also, I am turning over in my mind what I myself would have done with Chiquita's thousand dollars. Such a splendid sum of money!

Then I stop thinking, and a warm, glad feeling comes over me. It's a dead cinch that I, Diego Cordoniz, would have done a magnificent thing. For a woman of such understanding nothing would been too good.

When I awake, it is in terror that this is already the mañana when I have promised the truck. Before the morning is started, a neighbor drives into the yard and Juan is asked to help with the calving of a cow. They have gone off in a cloud of dust. Chiquita is left hoeing in the garden, and myself poking carrots to the rabbits. It is a bad situation.

"When do you think he will come back?" I ask.

"I wouldn't even guess," she answers. "You would have to ask the cow."

Time is short. "How much," I ask, "do you think this flock of miserable chickens is worth,"

"A few hundred dollars," she says, hoeing along. "Why?"

"What would you give," I continue, "to see Juan take a contract on the sea wall and make a lot of money?"

"Don't you ever give up?" she laughs.

"Would you give these chickens?" I ask.

"Of course. He is always complaining of them anyway."

"I suppose he owns these chickens in the clear?" I ask cautiously.

"He ought to," she says, "we raised them ourselves."

"The saints be praised!" I exclaim. Then I tell her the thing that is in my mind. The magnificent thing. "We will sell these lousy chickens at the poultry store for a few hundred dollars! With this money we will buy you a thousand dollars' worth of beautiful things — a radio, a washing machine, a sewing machine, a fur coat. We can make down payments on everything!"

Her eyes shine like silver conchas. Her lips tremble. "We would not dare," she breathes. "He would skin us alive."

"But you would have the things he wants you to have," I argue. "It will be paying you back your investment."

"We should speak to him first," she says.

"I was going to," I point out. "Now he is gone."

She frowns. I see she is full of doubt. Finally she throws down her hoe. "Diego Cordoniz," she cries, "can you drive the truck?"

In my joy I would like to lift her from the ground with a great hug. "I am a truck skinner from way back," I boast. I do not mention that I have no driver's license. I will find my cousin's if he has left it behind.

"I have an extra key to the ignition," she tells me. "If only he doesn't come back too soon!"

It is a morning to remember all my life. With a long pole with a sliding wire loop on the end, we catch all the chickens save a few which are left to eat. I make partitions of old boards and the canvas, which will not be needed now, in the truck. Doing a magnificient thing goes quickly. Chiquita has changed her dress. In no time we are singing down the highway.

Only once does she become afraid. "What about the monthly payments on the things we are going to buy?" she asks.

"One thing at a time," I reply. She is busy with a pencil and list. She needs only to be reassured. "The main thing now," I point out, "is to sell these insignificant birds."

My cousin's wife trades with the sharpness of a butcher's knife. When she comes from the poultry store she is folding two hundred and eighty dollars into her purse.

"Now we will go to the biggest department store," she commands, "where everything can be got at once."

Because we have the truck, our things can be loaded as they are bought. I see to this while she is in the office paying down. In a few hours there is not money enough between us even for a sandwich.

"We have cold enchiladas at home," she says happily. "It is wonderful what you can buy with a few hundred dollars."

"I hope you bought a thousand dollars worth."

She takes a paper from her purse. It is ugly with much fine print. "A thousand, fifty-five dollars worth," she informs me, "and twenty-three cents, to be exact." There is on her face the bliss of a beautiful animal in the middle of a scratching. "I have everything I want," she sighs. "even if Juan beats us both, it will be worth it."

This is the thought I do not like. My cousin is a bigger man than I am. "Perhaps," I say uncertainly, "it will not occur to him."

When we arrive, he is nowhere to be seen. By backing the truck to the porch, I can slide everything out without trouble. I pray the cow will delay matters indefinitely.

With a rug and floor lamps, the house is a new place. The radio is like a shining little casket. The washing machine goes to the kitchen and the portable sewing machine to the bedroom. Beside the stove I put the soft chair which Chiquita has bought for my cousin. When we are finished, I drop into this chair like a dead man.

But Chiquita is fairly dancing up and down.

"I can't wait to put it on," she is saying, as she unties the box she has been hugging all the way home. She lifts out a fur coat and dives into it. She is standing like a million dollars on the hoof.

"You should have had that long ago—" I start to say. Then I stop.

My cousin stands in the door. He is fresh from the cow, and his sleeves are rolled up. Because he has seen the truck, he is reciting the names of many saints and animals. Then his eyes pop at Chiquita. He sees the other things.

"Surprise! Surprise, darling!" Chiquita cries.

When she has stopped kissing him, we guide him to the soft chair. I swing my hand wide. It is a gesture to inspire confidence. "More than a thousand dollars' worth of fine things! My cousin, you said I was crazy. But I have got this money, and we have already spent it!"

He jumps and runs about. He sees the washer and the sewing machine. He turns on the radio and bounces up and down on the soft chair. He is beside himself.

"Dog of a dog!" he cries. "What has happened?"

"A stroke of good business," I say grandly. "Now we can be on our way to the sea wall." I hand him back his driver's license, which has been taken taken from his coat in the bedroom.

"But how did you do it?"

"A certain party—" I begin.

"All these beautiful things!" Chiquita cries. She flops on his lap and tickles his ears with the fur coat. "I am so happy! Say you are happy, too, my wonderful Juanito!"

"Sure, I'm happy," he says. He looks at me in wonder. "But, Diego, my cousin, you should not have done this. You should not have spent your money."

"It was nothing," I say unhappily.

All at once he grabs Chiquita. "You told him about our business!" he accuses her.

It is a thing I have not seen before. Chiquita becomes like a sick little squirrel in his arms. A weeping ball of fur. She explains to him about the chickens.

My cousin is without strength. He sits like a man struck with a sash weight. "At least we won't have to feed them," he says at last. His mouth moves some more, but no words come out.

"What is it, Juanito?" Chiquita asks.

"The payments!" he moans. "You have loaded me with more payments!"

But he has missed the whole point. "These payments are owing only to a department store," I exclaim, "an institution which means nothing. Besides, two hundred eighty dollars are already paid down. No more is necessary for a long time."

"Now the truck is all yours," Chiquita whispers to him. "My investment is out of it."

"Yesterday," I remind him, "we made a deal. I have secured the money I promised. We have only to form our company and begin operations. Come, my cousin —"

It is already afternoon, and the boss will be thinking that I, Diego Cordoniz, am another big liar. I have said *mañana*, and *mañana* is about gone.

My cousin stares at his toes. He scratches his head. He gets out a small pencil and a piece of paper. He wets the pencil on his tongue.

"How much did all this cost?" he scowls.

"A thousand and fifty-five dollars."

"And twenty-three cents," Chiquita adds.

He writes it down while she is looking everywhere for the paper with the fine print.

"Less two hundred and eighty dollars paid down," I remind him.

"*Huy!*" he grunts, as he subtracts.

Over his shoulder I see he has come to $775.23. "There!" I say. "It is less than Chiquita's thousand dollars. You cannot deny it."

"It is true," he gives in. "It is less than her part of the truck."

"Besides, you have no lousy chickens to feed every day!"
This is an angle he himself has mentioned. "How many sacks
of feed did they eat in a year? Figure the cost."

He waves me aside. He puts down the figures for the bank
and the finance company. Finally he is a man whipped by his
own arithmetic.

"Diego," he grins, "you are one smart *hombre*. I owe two
hundred twenty-four dollars, seventy-seven cents less than I
did yesterday."

Yet I do not like the way he says this. There is a little edge
to it. It is possible I have done too much of a smart thing. I have
poked my nose into his business. Perhaps he feels that I have
caused Chiquita to work against him. Or perhaps his dignity
requires that he, too, do a magnificent thing. The mind of a
Cordoniz is full of corners. But when he stands up, I think, for
a certainty, he is about to stick out his hand and thank me.

"Diego," he begins, "you have done a good and generous
thing for which I love you—"

"It was nothing," I protest.

"We will be partners and take a contract on the sea wall.
We will use the truck."

These are the beautiful words for which I have been
waiting. "You will bless the day!" I answer happily.

"But there is one thing." A darkness settles on my cousin's
face, and he puts his nose close to mine.

Because I am looking to his eyes, I do not see the hand that
has become a fist until it is almost too late.

"Juan! No!" Chiquita cries. Suddenly she is hanging to his
arm. "Cousin Diego is your friend! He needed your help!"

"You should not have sold my chickens," my cousin mutters to me. "Every time I think of it, I will want to sock you."

"Dog of a dog!" I cry. "How else was I to get a thousand
dollars?"

"You certainly had a nerve!" he growls. "But perhaps I will
not think of it very often." He offers now to shake with me,

and I am in a bad trap for sure. I give him my hand and shut my eyes. When he squeezes, my knuckles explode like popcorns. "One Cordoniz should always help the other," he forgives me. "Who do we see now to get this hauling contract?"

In no time we are all in the truck, going at a bad rate. Chiquita is wrapped to the ears in her fur coat, and Juan is pushing the gas to the floor. Four Saint Christophers are not too many. It is a ride to forget. When we skid to a stop at the sea wall, even the boss sticks his head from the shack to see what the trouble is.

When I speak to him, his sad face is even sadder. To him this life is a bad hang-over.

"Where did you come from?" he asks. "Who's the rabbit in the truck? What's the idea of raising a big rumpus?"

I present Chiquita and my cousin Juan. I explain that I, Diego Cordoniz, am a man of my word. I have returned with a truck.

The boss does not believe it. "Let's see the registration slip," he demands. He talks to Chiquita and Juan. But his opinion of me, I think, is much improved because of my connections. "It's a deal," he says finally. "I'll fix up a contract, and you can start in the morning."

I am tired as a man returned home from a rough trip. While they settle a price, I listen to the big waves smacking the rocks in the distance. It is a sweet and natural music. Suddenly Chiquita jabs me with her elbow.

The boss is saying, "If you and your cousin here are partners, I guess you don't want your old job back."

I am struck with fright. "Wait, boss! I've got to have my job back! You promised me!"

My cousin surveys me with a great suspicion in his eyes.

It is only when the boss assures me that I am working for the company again that I breathe with comfort.

When the three of us are alone, I explain. "It is no small thing to direct where a rock is to be put. It is important to select a safe place where a truck is to be backed. I will keep our truck away from the edge. If there is an accident, it will not be to us."

They are full of admiration. "Diego, you are not so dumb," Juan beams.

"Maybe someday," Chiquita says, "we will have dozens of trucks."

But it is not in my character to be ambitious. "One truck is enough," I observe happily. "With care, this job will last as long as there is an ocean."

—

MURDER IN THE HARBOR

"I live on Pico Street and I am called Gonzalez," my uncle says respectfully. "This boy is Pedro, the son of my brother who is called José."

"Your first name?" the policeman asks.

"Luis."

"And the number on Pico Street?"

"There is no number," Uncle Luis answers. "She is on the alley. A one-room house which belongs to Fernando Gomez. His daughter, Rosa, is married to Sam Hondo, who has the garage."

"No number," the policeman says. "Where do you work?"

"Work?" Uncle Luis smiles. "It is bad enough to be poor, *señor!*"

"Where can we find you when we want you?"

"After my morning coffee I am often at Manual Velez's barbershop," Uncle Luis replies with patience. "She is a place known to all. You are acquainted with her?"

"What do you do there?" the officer growls.

"I sit with my friends," my uncle replies with dignity. "Is there a law against that?"

"I suppose your brother sits there too?" the officer observes. "And the squirt here too?"

"She is a very pleasant place," my Uncle Luis answers, "and my nephew is not a squirt."

My Uncle Luis does not like people to make fun of me because I am small for my ten years. He is beginning to stand heavier, with his chin pulled lower against his neck. I think this policeman would be smart to lay off my Uncle Luis before he finds where the turtle puts his head.

"I'm told you spend a lot of time out here on the pier," the cop says. "Why? What do you do around here?"

My uncle shrugs. "One must eat, *señor*." He looks out to the breakwater and over the many fishing boats riding at the buoys in the Santa Monica harbor. When my Uncle Luis stops talking, there is a big hole in the air.

"We fish here," I explain, when he stays clammed up. "My uncle has a grappling hook which he uses to pull small salvage from the sea. When my father has no lawns to cut, he is often with us. If we did not fish maybe sometimes we would starve."

"What about your mother? Where does she work?" This copper's eyes light up as if he has connected with something big.

There is a growl in my Uncle Luis' throat. He takes my arm as if we have to be on our way. "Pay no attention to him," he says.

"You'd better pay attention!" the cop snaps. "Where's the boy's mother?"

"She ran away with a lettuce picker from the Imperial Valley!" I say angrily. "Is there anything else you'd like to nib-nose into?"

The cop swallows and looks at me with his black eyebrows pulled together in a big storm. "Sorry, kid. That's tough." He sticks his book and pencil back in his shirt pocket, and shakes out a cigarette, which he offers to my Uncle Luis.

"No, thank you," Uncle Luis replies stiffly.

"There's this much about it," the cop says: "A lot of valuable gear has been missing off those boats out there in the harbor. Just last night the Morelia's net was stolen. Maybe it's a gang, and you're working with them. Maybe not. But get this: Whoever it is, we'll put the finger on him! So think it over." He climbs on his motorcycle and kicks over the engine. "I'm checking up on you and your barbershop pals," he says.

When he is gone, my Uncle Luis makes a fist and bangs it against the pipe railing. "Why do they not find the deck hand from the Morelia?" he explodes. "The whole pier is whispering that Kurzy Lander has stolen the net and disappeared down the coast, maybe to San Diego where he came from. Why do they always jump on me when something is missing someplace?"

"Because you are a good one to jump on," I say, "and you know it."

"So I was born human enough to sin a little sometimes," he replies. "But in this case the police are very stupid. I cannot swim, and how would I get out the the Morelia?"

"Maybe you took somebody's rowboat from the racks under the pier," I say, "the same way you get out to the breakwater at night to catch lobsters sometimes."

"You are without perception," he replies. "It is a service to wet the bottom of a skiff, which will crack open if it is left to dry out." He uncoils the rope attached to the lead shank of our small grappling hook with its three long barbs, and lowers the hook carefully beside a piling. If he can find a mess of sinkers or a lost fishing rod perhaps we can sell them to buy something for our breakfast.

"That was a new cop," I say. "We have never seen him on the pier before."

"I know," he sighs. "A new cop is the worst kind. Until they get used to people, they are very objectionable."

My uncle is an old headache to the police, but he has never been in jail. One should never become attached to portable property, he has often said. An object which becomes a worry should be got rid of at once. The best things are those which are big enough to give pleasure, but are too small to stir envy and suspicion in others. In his pocket he always carries a walnut to prove this point to people. "In this shell is a great tree," he informs them, "but only a silly squirrel would envy me such wealth."

"Hey, Luis!" It is a shout from the Harbor Office on the deck above us. Captain Harker, the harbor master, stands in the door at the head of the ladder, his pipe clamped in his teeth. "Throw your hook by that piling next to the gas dock," he says. "Some jerk dropped a reel in there yesterday."

Uncle Luis wheels with a big smile. "*Gracias!*" he says. "Our stomachs could use such a piece of bad luck."

"How'd you make out with the police?" the harbor master asks.

My uncle shrugs and spits over the railing. "A friend of yours?" he asks.

The harbor master shrugs back. He is the biggest man I know. He has been a great sea captain, and it is said on the pier that his papers are good on all the oceans of the world. In my Uncle Luis' book he is one man who can see through a fog.

"A wind from the southeast," Uncle Luis calls up to him.

"Better batten down your hatches, *amigo*," Captain Harker replies, and goes back inside his office.

"A fine man," Uncle Luis whispers to me. "If he caught us stealing from a boat he would send us both to Alcatraz."

Uncle Luis pulls up a few starfish which are worth nothing and a rusty bucket full of mud. He leans over the edge and throws the hook under the pier.

The next minute he lets out a word which is bad even in Spanish. "I think I'm snagged!" he shouts, and heaves on the rope. "I have hooked into a chunk of seaweed."

"Wait!" I cry. I slide like a monkey over the side of the pier and down the ladder where the lifeguard boat is riding between her lines. Underneath are the wide crosspieces that brace the pilings. If I can get to Uncle Luis' rope, maybe I can pull it loose from the seaweed. I have done it many times before.

Under the pier, small waves slap a few feet below the heavy timber on which I crawl to the rope. It is already stretched tight. Uncle Luis is pulling above, and I brace my feet and heave with him. The rope gives a little, but it is hooked into something heavy which does not want to move.

"Pull harder!" I shout.

Suddenly, whatever it is begins to come, a few inches at a time. It is big and dark, and soft to the hook, like a great bunch of kelp, but the hook does not tear loose the way it would from kelp. I leave the pulling to Uncle Luis and flop down on my stomach to see deeper into the water.

It is a net. I can see the meshes now as clear as anything. If it is the stolen net from the Morelia, it can hold many tons of fish and is worth more money than an automobile.

"Harder!" I cry. I am up and pulling on the rope like crazy. For finding this net there will be a big reward and we will all be rich. We can eat all the time. I can hardly wait to look again. When it touches the edge of sunlight I almost fall off the timber, I am so happy.

Then I think I am seeing crazy. My stomach feels as if there is a sick pelican inside. There is a dead man tangled in the net. His hand is sticking up as white as paper and I can count the fingers.

"Help! Uncle Luis, help!" I hang on to the piling and scream that I have found something terrible.

It is only a minute before Uncle Luis has tied the rope to the pipe railing and is down the ladder. He looks where I point into the water.

"*Por Dios*," he whispers. "It is a floater." He gets down on his hands and knees to see deeper and examine what is below us. "Pedro," he says finally, "this man is Kurzy Lander, and it's the net from the Morelia, all right."

"We must tell somebody quick!" I cry. "We must tell Captain Harker!" I have never seen a drowned man before, and I am scared.

"It is not so simple," he replies.

"But we must do something!"

"The thing to do is to get our hook loose," he growls. "This is a bad thing to be connected with."

"You're not—not just going to leave him?"

"This man was killed," he answers. "A man does not get wrapped in a net and sunk under the pier by himself." He begins to pull at the hook and tries to work it loose.

"Be careful," I whisper.

"If our hook is found in this net, it will go bad with us!" he pants. "Maybe somebody is already watching us! Whoever killed this man is not far away! There are many eyes on this pier! If it is known that we found this thing, you know what will happen?"

"What?"

"This!" He slashes his finger across his throat, and makes a dead-duck squawk in his back teeth. "Just like that!"

"But if we tell Captain Harker!" I beg.

"May we live so long!" he says. "If only this dog of a hook would let go!" He goes out on another timber to pull the hook from a new direction.

"Luis! Hey, Luis!" It is my father's voice calling softly over the edge of the pier. "Are you down there?"

"Here we are," Uncle Luis replies in a loud whisper. "Are you alone, José?"

"Sí!"

"Come down quick! We have found something! Be careful you are not seen!"

It is perhaps five minutes before my father comes inching along the timbers from another direction. He is a thin man and when he moves slowly he can hardly be told from the shadow of a piling.

When he reaches us his face is sad with worry. He holds up his hand to keep my Uncle Luis quiet. "This is a very bad place to hide," he says. "I came as fast as I could. The police have been to Manuel Velez's barbershop. He said you had gone to look for uranium in the Kern River Valley. Jesús Rinaldo told them you were in Fresno picking grapes. I had already said you were in San Diego to see the animals in the zoo. Believe me, Luis—"

"*Caramba!* Will you shut up and listen!" my uncle explodes. "We have found a dead man in the stolen net from the Morelia!"

While Uncle Luis explains everything, my father gently pushes the hair from my forehead.

"If we tell Captain Harker—" I break in.

"Quiet!" Uncle Luis shuts me off. "If the police think I am mixed up in this, José, no telling what they might dig up on me. If the murderer finds out we have seen this thing, he will kill us, too, to keep our mouths shut."

My father feels in his watch pocket for the small tin box in which he carries cigarette butts. "Luis," he says, "did you have anything to do with stealing this net from the Morelia?"

"I swear I did not even know it until this morning!"

My father's eyes light up, and there is a change over his face like the sun from behind a cloud. "But the police—" he says doubtfully.

"If city hall is missing, they look in my pocket first," Uncle Luis replies. He is still yanking on the hook, but it will not come free.

"Here," my father says. "Give me the rope. A hook is like a woman. Sometimes when you want her to come, you must first let her go." He jiggles the rope and lets it go loose so the hook will sink to the bottom. In a few minutes he has untangled it from the net. But when he turns from the water his face looks as if he will be sick. "I hope I did not touch anything I shouldn't," he says.

"Blessed Virgin!" Uncle Luis cries. "Let's get out of here!" He motions that I should go first and see that it is safe for us.

The top of the ladder beside the lifeboat is at the corner of the pier. It can be seen from the Harbor Office and the Lifeguard Office on the upper deck. But the lifeguards are not in sight, and Captain Harker is at the other corner of the pier, bossing men who are painting the keel of the harbor tug. Only a few sleepy fishermen are on the benches. I signal it is all clear.

When they are beside me, my father warns we must think this thing through. "A good place," he says, "is on the pile of lumber in back of the merry-go-round at the other end of the pier."

Suddenly Uncle Luis grabs my arm with one hand and begins to push my father with the other. "Watch out," he whispers.

Two fishermen carrying poles are walking fast from the door of the café, as if they are just waking up to something.

"Not so quick!" one says. He is an ugly customer who needs a shave and has a big scar across his forehead under the bill of his fishing cap. The other man is a skinny jerk in blue sailor pants and a dirty sweat shirt. They give us a couple of nasty grins and keep walking against us until we are pushed to the railing.

"What gives with you greasers under the pier?" the scar-head wants to know.

Uncle Luis breaks into a stream of Spanish. He manages to say we have been hunting starfish to sell to tourists. He is studying the scar-head as if he is a bad smell that he remembers from someplace before.

"What else you see down there besides starfish?" the skinny jerk wants to know.

"The water she is very deep," my father says. "Is nothing on the pilings. No mussels even."

"You got no business under there, you know that, don't you?" Scar-head barks. All at once he grabs my Uncle Luis by the shirt front. "I know you! They call you Luis! You're the guy was tryin' to peddle a hot radiator gismo in the Casa Grande bar one night."

"Correction!" My Uncle Luis brings the grappling hook from behind his back. I think if there is more trouble he will bury it in somebody's head. "That was an object I found in the street!" he says. "Remove the hands!" When Scar-head backs away, my Uncle Luis laughs without humor. "You should stick to driving a truck with illegal lobsters to Las Vegas," he observes.

Scar-head and the skinny one cannot take their eyes from the grappling hook. It is clear they are considering the wet rope and what we have been up to.

"Just lookin' for starfish, huh?" Scar-head says with an ugly sneer. "Just pokin' around, huh?"

"Excuse me!" I say, and start to move. I think if I can get over to the other side of the pier, where Captain Harker is, I will tell him everything before something happens.

"Oh, no, you don't!" Scar-head grabs me. He makes a nasty motion with his thumb as if he will scoop out my eye. He holds my head back by the hair. "You're scared stiff!" he grits. "What'd you find under the pier?"

"Don't do that," my father says softly. There is a little click in his coat pocket as he steps forward. Scar-head is a man who could hear such a sound of a snap knife in a boiler factory. He jerks his hand from my head. "We have some business to take care of," my father informs him. "Keep away from us."

The skinny man who has said nothing has produced a fish knife and is feeling the edge with his thumb. "I think you know something that you'd better forget," he says. "Don't go to no cops. And don't go to no confessions. You don't want somethin' should happen to the little shrimp here, now, do you?"

My father's face goes tight, and Uncle Luis stands very loose, as he does when there is great anger on him. It is the way he stood before he hit Paco Flores, who kicked the dog off Carmelita Smith's porch.

"Understand?" Scar-head asks. "You'll be watched. We'll get the kid, not you!"

"*Si*," my father says.

"We understand," Uncle Luis nods. "We also do not forget." He grips the hook, and my father's hand trembles at the edge of his pocket. We move away as if nobody is going to push us, and we will go when we please.

When we are on the lumber pile in back of the merry-go-round, my father says, "It is a lucky thing, Luis, they were in the café and did not see you and Pedro when you went under the pier."

"They are the murderers, all right," Uncle Luis answers. "They will be watching on the end of the pier until a boat comes in the night to the gas dock. It is very simple. They can hook onto the net from there without suspicion and pull it out into the channel and out to sea under water. Then they can load it and go away."

"And sink the body far out in the ocean," my father adds.

"It was a smart idea they had there to hide the net under the pier," Uncle Luis says. "It is the last place anybody would look. They must have pulled the net from the stern of the Morelia with a rowboat last night. They did not know the deck hand was aboard. There was a bad fight, and then they didn't know what to do with the body. So they wrapped him in the net."

"A terrible thing!" my father sighs. "They are evil men who will kill again if it is necessary. By now they have looked under the pier and seen the water on the timber where we pulled the rope up. They think we know already, but they will be sure when they see the wet place over the net."

"We must go to the police," I say. "I am not afraid."

"It is enough that we are afraid for you," my father answers.

"If the police find out now, no matter who tells them," Uncle Luis growls, "the murderers will think it was us. For myself I do not care, but—" He falls silent and pats my shoulder.

"Until they are caught, we are in great danger," my father says. "They cannot afford to trust us to keep our mouths shut. They will find some other way to make sure."

"Why—why—" I begin, and the thought which has come to me is almost to big to say.

"Yes, little one?" my father says gently.

"If we can't go to the police, we must catch the murderers ourselves and give them to the cops!"

My Uncle Luis looks at me as if I am ten feet tall. "You are a crazy kid! You are one to bite out the eyes of an octopus! *Caramba*, José! What a kid!"

"Now wait, Luis," My father says slowly. "Even a big whale can be taken with a small harpoon if it is done right."

"Sure, a whale maybe, but —" Uncle Luis groans and scratches his chin. Just the same, there is a light in his eye as he considers the possibility. "To hang it on them, the murderers must be caught red-handed with the goods," he says. "There will be more than two of them. This is a job which requires brains."

As my father and Uncle Luis talk, I am full of ideas which they tell me are not practical. I must use my head, they say. If the police could never catch my Uncle Luis with portable property, to catch two murderers with a net and a dead man will be even harder. We must try to figure every move they will make.

Finally, when my father is out of cigarette butts and Uncle Luis has trimmed all his toenails, it looks to everybody as if there is but one handle to the bucket after all. My father rubs his hand over my hair.

"Remember," he says, "you are but a boy. A boy cannot lift as much as a man. It is the same with facing danger. You understand? A little is enough."

"I am going to Sam Hondo's garage to use the grinding wheel," Uncle Luis says as he stands up. "The points must be sharp to take hold in hard timber."

"And I will speak privately with Manuel Velez at the barbershop," my father answers. To me he says, "You will look through the scrap piles around the pier to see what you can find. Then you will go to the top deck at the end of the pier and keep an eye on the murderers. Be careful you are not seen. If anything happens, come fast and Manuel will tell you where to find me."

"We will meet here again when the sun goes down," Uncle Luis says. "Until then, the less we are seen the better."

"Remember," my father warns me again, "keep out of sight."

I am lucky in finding what we need in the wood stored under the pier. Then I sneak out toward the end. Scar-head is just coming out of the phone booth at the head of the stairs above the café. When he has gone down on the lower deck, I hide where I can watch from behind some old buoys stacked near the boat hoist. The murderers do nothing but talk and drink from a bottle in a paper sack, but they are watching everybody all the time.

In the afternoon a small fantail boat goes by outside the breakwater. Scar-head makes a big deal of wiping his fishing rod with a white handkerchief. There is a toot from the boat whistle.

At five o'clock I see Captain Harker go home. In a little while the Harbor Office is empty, except for a night lifeguard, who sits with his feet on the switchboard and reads a book. A few people who think the fish bite at night are beginning to come. A traffic cop rides out and watches the fog bank roll in from the direction of Santa Catalina Island. When the lifeguard starts the foghorn, the cop cannot hear his radio, and he goes away. On the lower deck the man from the marine-supply store puts the lock on the gate of the fence around the gas pumps, and then leaves. The two murderers change their place to fish nearer the gas dock. When it is almost dark I can hardly see the breakwater and the boats. The cold fog is drifting between the pilings, and when I think of what is under the pier, it makes me shiver. I race all the way down the pier to the merry-go-round.

My father is waiting with a coat he has brought for me, and Uncle Luis has a sack of tortillas and onions. While I chew them down, I tell everything I have seen.

"The devil is with the murderers," Uncle Luis grumbles, "but we were right about the boat."

"Who knows?" my father says softly. "If they cannot be seen in the fog, neither can we." When he strikes a match to his cigarette, the light leaps from the long points of Uncle Luis' grappling hook, which he has ground sharp as needles.

"I have found good poles," I say proudly, and uncover what I have hidden in the lumber pile. "They are stakes for the sand fence which is being built near the parking lot."

"Nice redwood," my father says, bending one under his foot.

"The time for talk is over," Uncle Luis says, as he lifts the grappling hook and the rope. "They can be in and out with that boat in five minutes. We must get busy."

We keep to the edge of the buildings until we reach the ladder where the fish company has a loading hoist. My father hugs me around the shoulder.

"Remember," he says, "you are only a sea gull tonight. Make the sound twice and then once, so we will be sure."

I make the cry of the sea gull, which I can do as perfect as if I have feathers.

"Good!" Uncle Luis says. For the first time I can ever remember, he and my father shake hands.

"You on the shore side above the net, and I on the ocean side," my father whispers.

"And this in the middle!" Uncle Luis pats the hook, and his face is hard. "José, are you sure about Manuel Velez? If something has slipped, we are going to our own funerals."

"Manuel is our good friend," my father answers. "Because he has a business, he will be believed."

"May the saint of this day watch over us," Uncle Luis says. He makes a deep sound in his chest as he embraces me. The next minute they are over the side with the poles and the hook.

It is my job to watch near the gas dock. When the boat comes in, I must warn my father and Uncle Luis. The two murderers will have to come down under the pier to drop an anchor into the net so it can be dragged away. It is then I will cry like a gull. My father and Uncle Luis will be hidden on the timbers behind the pilings, with the long poles and the sharp grappling hook.

When I have slipped along the pier and down behind an overturned dory on the lower deck, I see that there is no light on the post at the gas dock. I think somebody has cut a wire. Scar-head and the skinny man are leaning over the railing near the ladder. The lifeguard boat has been taken away someplace, but the fog is so thick I cannot see where. There is a light in the Lifeguard Office on the upper deck, but I can see only the top of the head of the guy who is on the switchboard.

While I am holding my breath for something to happen, a terrible thought comes to me. There is a big hole in the plan we have made. If the boat does not come for the murderers and the net, my father and my Uncle Luis will go to prison as sure as I am little Pedro Gonzalez.

It was my Uncle Luis' big stupid idea to get my father to go to Manuel Velez and fix it for Manuel to go to the police station and be a stool pigeon. He was to say that my Uncle Luis and my father had the stolen net from the Morelia hidden under the pier. They were going to take it away after dark and sell it to a thief who would come with a boat from San Pedro. It was the idea to have the cops there when we had caught the murderers. Then we would not get our throats cut. But if this boat does not come, the police will capture only my father and Uncle Luis. They will go to prison as sure as anything, and the real murderers will get away.

I sneak from behind the dory to run to another part of the pier, where I can slip down underneath to tell them. It is then I see a gray thing in the fog on the other side of the pier which was not there before. It is the big Coast Guard boat without a light. Down the pier there are two cars which slip without lights to the side of the fish market. I am sure it is the police, and they have called the Coast Guard from San Pedro. Maybe the lifeguard boat is waiting out in the harbor too. If they turn the searchlights under the pier now, my father and Uncle Luis will be on their way to Alcatraz.

I do not know what to do. My lips are so stiff I think they will not make the cry of the sea gull, even if I want them to. If I gum things up now, my father and Uncle Luis will never forgive me. They have trusted me to do a job. All I know is, I must do it. As I creep back behind the overturned dory on the lower deck, I am so mad at the Coast Guard I could cry. If their boat has been spotted by the fantail job which is coming for the net, it is all over. The fantail could be ten miles away by now.

It is like waiting my whole life. Then I see a thing which raises hair on me all over. Scar-head is holding a flashlight under his hand and flashing it north across the harbor. Since the Coast Guard boat is on the south side, maybe it has not been seen. I pray to the saint of this day that the crazy police will be good for a little while longer, and that the fog is not too thick for the fantail to see the signal.

It is not long. Never have I seen a boat come so fast in a fog. There are no lights on her, and she slips down the second mooring lane like a big shark in dirty water. She slides past the gas dock and her engine purrs softly as she noses to the channel. She swings her fantail back into the corner between the dock and the pier.

Scar-head and the skinny man throw down their fishing rods and leap for the ladder. They grab a line which is thrown by a man on the stern. I give the cry of the sea gull. Twice, and then once.

There is a small anchor on the stern of the boat which is jerked into the water. Nobody has said a word. The anchor sinks in the boiling water behind the boat. Scar-head and the skinny one are underneath now, pulling it back into the net.

There is a terrible cry in the blackness, and a splash. Then another great groan, as if a man has been poked with a pile driver in the stomach. It is my father and Uncle Luis at work with the poles.

"Keep poking their heads under water!" Uncle Luis shouts. "I'll get the one on the boat!"

The next second there is a crash as the grappling hook flies from under the pier into the deckhouse glass of the boat. My Uncle Luis leaps to the fantail with his pole before him like a fish spear. A gun spits fire. The bullet zings through the wire of the gas-pump fence.

"Police! Police! Help!" I yell with all my lungs.

Suddenly everything is a blaze of light. The big beam from the Coast Guard boat cuts under the pier. Another shoots in from the harbor with the lifeguard boat, and the big searchlight from the harbor Office sweeps down on top of us. There are cops everywhere, and more uniforms than in a parade.

My Uncle Luis has his knee across the neck of the big slob on the boat, and will not get up until he is helped off by two uniforms from the Coast Guard. His arm is bleeding, and they tell him he will get first aid in a minute from the lifeguards.

"It is nothing!" he shouts. He runs to find his grappling hook in the deckhouse, and to untie the rope from the piling.

From underneath the pier my father is helped out by other men, who are patting him on the back until he is coughing and trying to get his breath.

In the excitement I think it is a good time to find the fishing rods of the two murderers and put them up inside under the seats of the overturned dory. We could use such rods, and they will not need them any more.

It is only after I have hidden the rods that I see Captain Harker has been watching me. I get hot all over. But he nods that it is O.K. He pretends he has seen nothing, and steps to where my Uncle Luis has been brought up and stands with my father while they wipe his arm and put on a bandage.

"A good night's work, *amigos!*" Captain Harker says.

"Maybe someday you will hire us to work in the harbor," my father says. "We have a feeling for such a life."

"*Señores! Señores!*" It is the high voice of Manuel Velez, and he is trying to tell eveybody he is not a stool pigeon and that he was only helping us to catch the murderers.

"Had it not been for this Manuel!" — Uncle Luis smiles at the police — "you would not have come looking for a mouse and caught three gorillas instead."

Down on the gas dock they are taking up the net with the dead man. The two murderers are pulled fighting from the water and the handcuffs put on.

A girl and a big man with a camera push into the crowd and inform everybody that they are from the press. They demand what everything is about and who is the hero and how everything happened.

It is my Uncle Luis who pushes me before everybody. "This is Pedro Gonzalez, who found the net and the body," he says. "The rest was only a small matter for my brother and myself."

When they have taken my picture with Uncle Luis and my father for the newspapers, I say to the man with the camera, please will he do something.

It is then then I am permitted to stand before Captain Harker, with my father and my Uncle Luis on each side of me. We have our pictures taken all together. Someday, when I am a great sea captain on all the oceans of the world, I will put this picture in the wheelhouse of my own ship.

SOMETHING FOR NOTHING

My cousin, Manuel Velez, the barber, and myself do not see eye to eye on many things. For example, Manuel knows little about women. Because he is close with his money, he has not learned much. For myself, I have an aching heart for Rosita Santee, but I would not go the length of myself for money. So it is a question, and our days in Santa Monica are full of argument.

Manuel is sitting now in his barber chair smoking his cigar and I am putting the brush to the brown shoes Rosita's father has left with me two hours ago. We are looking out on Pico Street. The sun has moved with the afternoon, and there is a small square of shade in front of the shop.

"Paco," my cousin says to his cigar, "the world is full of things I want. Sometimes I feel sorry for myself."

"It is the heat," I suggest, but I, too, am not at peace with my own mind, and do not believe what I am saying. For a long time now, Rosita has been after me to make something of myself, which is a way of saying she will not marry me until I have more money, perhaps a business of my own. She has offered to keep her job at the Castilian Kitchen and to help me. Because I was not born rich, I feel like a heel. She is more beautiful than the flowers in her own black hair, and I am not happy two steps away from her.

"Well, well! Another *turista!*" Manuel says, disturbing me from my thoughts.

A fat car with a small, canvas-covered trailer on two wheels has stopped in the street. It is a dirty car, and the windshield is full of stickers. A heavy gringo in a green wool shirt climbs out and wipes his face. He slams the door on the poor woman inside who holds a map. He walks around the trailer, and it is clear that something has happened which is about all he can take. He scowls at us as if we had insulted him.

"Is there a garage near here?" he demands.

"No. señor," Manuel says.

"Where's your telephone directory?"

"No telephone, señor," Manuel says.

"A hell of a place!" he snorts. "I've got a flat tire on my trailer."

"So?" Manuel observes through his cigar smoke. "An old tire, I suppose?"

"What's the difference?" the gringo shouts. "Who can I get to fix it?"

Manuel looks to me for an opinion. "Paco, do we know anybody in the neighborhood who could fix an old tire?"

I shrug. "Not this afternoon, señor."

The gringo walks to the curb and pulls open the door on the woman. "Marie, I'm through!" he shouts. "I'm fed up! This trailer business was your idea, but this ends it!"

He jerks the canvas from the trailer, and begins pushing things into the back of the automobile. There is a new tent and vacuum jug and stove. There is a skillet only a little black, blankets stuck full of foxtails, and folding beds and fishing poles. It does not take long to fill the car.

When he has all he can manage, he swears at what is left over and throws the canvas back on top of it. He kicks the pin from the tongue of the trailer. With an ugly laugh at Manuel and me and everything, he brushes his hands together and climbs into the car.

"I have thought sometimes I would like to travel," Manuel says, "but I see now it is not always the answer."

As the fat car jumps away from the curb, the woman sticks her hand from the window and waves to us. We both wave back, and when I look at Manuel again, there is a quick light in his eyes.

"A gift from the ravens," he says. "The Good Padre has not forgotten us."

"It is a good tire," I remark at the curb. "It is a fine trailer." Because there is an out-of-state license on the back, I pull down a corner of the canvas to cover it. Something which does not belong in California would awake the suspicion of the police, perhaps. "There are a couple of nice folding chairs under this canvas," I point out.

"We could use the canvas for an awning," Manuel replies. "The frame we have is no good without something on it."

Concerning the ravens, I feel that Manuel has said more than he knows. One could rent such a trailer for perhaps as much as three dollars a day. In a small way it would be a business, though perhaps not such a one as Rosita dreams about. Yet to be strictly honest my cousin is entitled to half, and that is a problem. Manuel, I hope, will not think of the rent idea himself, before I have found a way to handle the thing to better advantage. But I can see he is already considering the money possibilities of what we have here. "Perhaps they will come back for it," I suggest to discourage him.

"Not a chance," he answers. "You heard what the gringo said."

Señor La Paz, who cuts tombstones, appears suddenly out of nowhere for a razor he has left to be sharpened, and Jesús Rinaldo, who is no longer working at the shipyard, slips out of the shade from across the street.

"I know a certain party who could use that trailer," he says.

When he is not reading the picture books in our shop, this Jesús Rinaldo spends much time in Gardena trying his luck at a poker palace which he calls "the laundry." Anything which is not nailed down sets his mind to going.

Señor La Paz observes, "I would like that trailer to haul headstones in. My son is looking around for one." He shakes his head over the flat tire.

I am wondering how many people have seen what has happened to us, when Luis Gonzalez moves from behind a palm tree. Luis is a man of many ideas who fishes small salvage from the pier with a grappling hook. He is a person without desire, and can be trusted in matters of judgment.

"What do you think of the trailer?" I ask.

For a long time he stands studying the situation. "You could make a shoe-shine wagon out of it," he says finally. "You could travel around the apartment houses and shine shoes. You could make a million dollars." He smiles at us. He shrugs his shoulders. "But who wants a million dollars anymore? I would say it should be sold, and the money spent to make people happy."

My heart has jumped in my chest at his idea of the shine wagon. With such a shoeshine business I could reap a harvest and marry my Rosita. I understand with Luis that money itself is nothing, but I know, too, that for me my Rosita is everything.

"That is something to consider," I say carefully, but already I see a shine wagon instead of a trailer, and it is a beautiful thing.

There is much small talk back and forth which means nothing, but I see in all faces that there is a desire to share in our good fortune. Presently Señor La Paz goes off muttering with his razor, and Jesús Rinaldo thinks of business elsewhere, giving a long look to the curb from the side of his eyes as he leaves. Luis Gonzalez helps himself to my cigarette papers and tobacco, and strolls away down the street. It occurs to me that he will report the trailer to his brother, José, and they will think about it. José, who cuts lawns, will think he could haul his tools around in such a trailer. To put it bluntly, I am afraid that since we have got something for nothing, all of Pico Street will be looking for a way to help us take care of it.

My cousin, Manuel, has been very silent. "Paco," he says finally, "possession is nine points of the law. I think we'd better bring those chairs into the shop and put up that awning before something happens to it." He, too, I think, has been considering that we have many friends.

I am quick to agree, and when we have the canvas tied on the frame with strong knots, we roll the trailer out of the street and far back alongside the shop under the window of our room.

"If anybody touches it, we will hear him," Manuel points out.

Even with a flat tire, the trailer rolls like a bicycle. It is indeed a fine, well-constructed vehicle, and with a few boards could be made into a magnificent shine wagon. I could push it anywhere, and in every big apartment house there would be hundreds of shoes, just waiting. Maybe later I could get another one, and hire another man, perhaps on commission.

My cousin thumps his hand on the flat tire. "Paco," he says with inspiration, "if Sam Hondo comes by tomorrow, we should have him fix this tire. It is not good to have so much dead weight on a flat inner tube."

Sam Hondo has a garage many blocks up Pico Street, but he sometimes stops at our shop on his way to the beach where his father-in-law, Señor Gomez, operates the merry-go-round. He could fix it right from his truck.

"Manuel," I say soberly, "what would you say your interest in this trailer is worth? What would you take for your part?"

"It's not for sale," Manuel answers. "Why?"

"I want it for myself," I confess.

Manuel surveys me thoughtfully. "Luis Gonzalez had a good idea there with that shine wagon," he says. "Don't think it slipped by me."

"But, Manuel, you understand why it is! You have a business—a nice little shop. I must have a business too."

"That Rosita!" Manuel says with disgust. "We have a good fifty-fifty proposition here. Besides, where would you get the money to buy me out? I must think about it."

"When I'm making money I can pay you off," I protest.

"When you are making money, my cousin, the interest will be worth more," Manuel answers.

His point is a good one. "Think it over, anyway," I say in despair. "And I will speak to Rosita. It is possible she will not like the idea at all."

But when I see my Rosita in the evening, and tell her everything, she throws her arms around my neck and kisses me as if I am already a big success.

"That Manuel!" she cries. "He has kept you under his thumb long enough! I have some money saved and we will buy him out together."

There, I think to myself, *I would only be trading thumbs.* "No," I say, "I will find a way by myself."

We are sitting on a box at the edge of the open-air picture show for people in automobiles, where Rosita's brother is hired to watch the parking and who lets us in free. She squeezes my hand in the dark, and I make a promise to myself that before I am through I will have a hundred shine wagons operating all over Los Angeles. What is bad is that I do not yet have the first one.

When I arrive home, my heart still pounding and my head spinning from the goodnight my Rosita has given me, I find my cousin fast asleep. His bare foot sticks from the covers, and to it is tied a string. I follow this string through the window and see that it is fastened outside to the trailer. My cousin, Manuel, is a quick thinker.

In the morning we are awake early. My cousin complains that he has not rested well for keeping an eye on the trailer. For lack of sleep, my own brain feels the size of a pea. But when we have had our coffee and opened the shop, and Manuel unfolds the two chairs that belonged to the *turista*, I say bluntly, "Rosita is all for me going into the shine-wagon business. What is the least you will take?"

There is an old watermelon seed stuck to the wooden arm of the canvas chair, and he picks it off with his nail file. "No deal," he says. "Either we have a partnership or I take a percentage. Business is business."

While we are talking, Rosita's father, Señor Santee, from the poultry store, comes in for his brown shoes, and he is all smiles.

"I hear you have had some good luck," he says. "At least there should be a haircut on the house." He climbs into the barber chair. "Take your time, Manuel," he says, and I consider, with a laugh inside me, that Rosita has put him up to this.

At this moment little Pedro Gonzalez comes snooping around on his way to school. Manuel sends him off to see if he can find Sam Hondo to fix the tire, in case he is going by.

Pedro is hardly out of sight when his uncle, Luis Gonzalez, and his father, José, appear. They sink with great weariness into the new chairs of the *turista*.

"No lawns to cut today, José?" Manuel asks suspiciously.

"I am in a mood for a haircut," José smiles, rolling a cigarette. "Perhaps also a shine."

Luis says nothing, but leans back, and his eyes rest with a long meditation on the canvas.

This is no more than is to be expected, perhaps, but when Señor La Paz and Jesús Rinaldo also show up, I am beginning to get worried.

"That razor you sharpened has a nick in it," Señor La Paz complains. "I will wait while you grind it out."

"Another hot day," Jesús Rinaldo yawns. "My room is already a bake oven." He stretches himself in the cool of the shop. "I would not like to be a *turista* traveling on such a day," he observes.

Since our shop is not large, by the time Señor Padilla, who keeps the dry-cleaning store across from us, comes in, there is not a vacant chair, so he climbs on my shine box.

"Fix 'em up," he says. "Nice day today, but maybe not so good as yesterday."

The thoughts that are filling my mind now have become a misery to me. Perhaps somebody has informed the police about the trailer. Maybe they are here to see what happens and ask a reward for stolen property.

"I observed what happened yesterday," Señor Padilla is saying as he studies the new chairs. "I have been told that last night the gringo stayed in town at the Casa del Mar hotel, where my brother is janitor. This morning he was eating his breakfast while the car was being greased. The wife is now out buying souvenirs." He pauses and glances from the side of his eyes at Manuel. "I wonder what the gringo is thinking about this morning?"

A shadow crosses my cousin's face, but he does not stop on Señor Santee's hair. "You do not know all the facts," he says smoothly, "or you would not worry yourself about what belongs to another."

At this moment Sam Hondo appears outside in his truck and shouts that he has been told we have a tire to fix. When we go out to show him about it, the others follow to the edge of shade under the awning. Sam gets his tools from the truck, but he is in no hurry.

"I can work better where it is cooler," he says, and before we can say no, he has the trailer in front under the awning.

More and more it presses on my mind that my cousin and I are in the middle of great trouble, and it is only a matter of time. It is the stillness before a cloudburst.

When Luis Gonzalez speaks, it is like the first few drops of rain. "If I had my life to live over," he says, "I would not own even the clothes on my back. In this world nothing is worth having but good friends."

Presently Manuel turns on the small radio which he keeps behind him in the towel closet.

"Turn it softer," Señor Padilla requests. "If there is a police siren, I want to hear it."

Señor La Paz slaps at a fly. Jesús Rinaldo stretches his legs. A bad restlessness moves in the others.

"On my birthday there was wine for everybody," José says dreamily. "If I remember, Manuel, it was you who brought it."

"Time changes a man," Luis reproves him. "The more one has, the more one wants."

"One will have nothing unless he shares it," Jesús Rinaldo says darkly.

Suddenly I see what is the trouble, and it is a thing to cheer me. They are all thinking how it can be possible to share in our good fortune, and they have come to a dead end. But in my hope I have reckoned without Jesús Rinaldo.

"A trailer presents a problem," he observes in the silence. "There is only one way to answer it, and that is to set up a trailer corporation."

I look to my cousin fearfully, and see that he is far from happy. He has climbed into his barber chair, and sits now like a king watching the revolution. He is considering how to save the pieces, but he knows it is a losing proposition.

"It is a bad time for corporations," he objects. "Besides, there are many conditions."

"We will consider them," Luis Gonzalez nods. He is studying Jesús Rinaldo with some respect.

"Paco must be president and I must be treasurer," Manuel says firmly. "We must have control."

"Nobody should control," Luis answers.

"That's right. You are outvoted," Jesús Rinaldo declares. "But since the shop will make a good main office, it is okay to be president and treasurer." He looks around at the others. "Okay, officers elected?"

"Okay!" they nod.

"What is a corporation?" José Gonzalez asks gently.

Jesús Rinaldo looks on him with pity. "In the shipyard I belonged to the union," he says. "It was explained all about corporations. It is very simple."

While we watch, he tears the front page from last Sunday's funny paper and lifts the scissors from Manuel's pocket. "It is impossible to divide up the trailer," he says, "so we will divide up the paper."

"That is a quick idea," Señor Santee smiles.

"We are nine men present," Jesús Rinaldo says when he has counted. "I will cut out nine pieces of paper, and we will divide the profits from operations nine ways."

It occurs to me that Jesús Rinaldo has been thinking of this thing all night, and I see I am losing my trailer, not to one Manuel but to nine people.

"What are the pieces of paper for?" José asks.

"They are shares of stock, my stupid friend," Jesús Rinaldo informs him as he hands the papers around. "For each share of stock, one piece of profits."

"This is not fair," Luis Gonzalez says. "Paco and Manuel have done more than we have in this matter. Give them each another piece of paper," he instructs.

He is a just man, this Luis, and will not see his friends robbed.

"But that cuts the profits in eleven pieces," Jesús Rinaldo objects. "Who can divide by eleven?"

"I can," Señor Santee says. "I will assist Manuel, the treasurer, when the time comes."

Jesús Rinaldo snips out another picture each for Manuel and me. "There is one picture left," he says quickly. "I will take it for making the organization. Twelve is a better number. We will call this corporation The Pico Street Transportation Company. No objection? Carried!"

"Not so fast!" Luis Gonzalez objects. "This is not a union meeting."

"What about the guy who left this thing?" Sam Hondo speaks with a worried face. "Have we got clear title?" Since he deals with automobiles, Sam is suspicious about titles.

"That is no problem," Luis informs him. "This is the same thing as salvage in the ocean."

Suddenly my cousin, Manuel, stiffens in the barber chair. I follow his look to the street, and I see what it is that has made his eyes pop. It is the end of everything. A fat car has eased up and wheeled around in the street. For a fact, it is the *turista*, and he has his wife beside him.

"The gringo!" Manuel whispers. He leaps from the chair as the big tires slide against the curb.

"He will have to fight the corporation," Jesús Rinaldo says through his teeth, and after that, except for the flies, there is not a movement in the shop. The corporation has become painted to the furniture.

For a few seconds the *turista* stands on the sidewalk like a bull in the chute. When he comes, it is not for a haircut.

"This is my trailer!" he shouts. "This is my stuff!"

"I beg pardon, señor," my cousin says, and shakes out the cloth as if he expects the gringo to climb into the chair. Sometimes he is a cool number, my cousin.

The gringo waves to the awning. "That's my canvas! What's it doing up there?" He sees the chairs under Luis and José, and his face becomes a worse purple. "Who's responsible for this?" he cries.

Manuel shrugs. "It is the corporation, señor," he apologizes. "You must take it up with the corporation."

"Corporation?" the gringo cries. "What corporation?"

"The Pico Street Transportation Company, señor," Jesús Rinaldo speaks up. "You understand about corporations, señor?"

"I own them!" the gringo explodes. "Where is this outfit?" He glares at us.

Luis is suddenly full of sorrow as he addresses the gringo. "You have a good question there, señor. Where is a corporation? I myself was just wondering the same thing."

"It's a legal entity, you fool!" the *turista* cries.

"Of course," I say with inspiration. "You must take up the matter of your trailer with this legal entity, señor."

"Is everybody here crazy?" shouts the gringo. "Get my stuff together and let me out of here! Or must I call the police?"

"I would not do that," Jesús Rinaldo says softly. "We are many witnesses to this thing."

While he is speaking, the gringo's wife has slipped from the car and is standing outside by the trailer where she can hear.

"It is not a thing to be angry about, señor." Luis Gonzalez speaks sadly. "Yesterday you went off and left your property, señor, like so much salvage. It was fished from the street and now belongs to the corporation. It is a pity, señor, but that's the way it is."

"Damn your corporation!" says the gringo, but not so loud this time.

"Pardon me, señor," I speak up bravely, "but yesterday we have heard you say that you were through. You were fed up. Everything was ended. When the señora waved to us, it was as much as to say 'Goody-by forever!' to the trailer. My cousin and I waved back, and it was like, what you might say, a bargain."

"I really did mean it that way, George!" It is the señora who speaks now. "Really, I did!"

The gringo wipes his face as if he is squeezing out a sponge. "Will you keep out of this, Marie?"

"But you weren't going to come back, you know," the señora insists. "It was only when I said the police could trace the license and find us in Detroit, and write, and make you pay freight—"

"Will you please, dear, shut up?" the gringo says, and he is sweating like a man found guilty.

Because it is in my mind that my Rosita is a little like the good señora, I make a suggestion. "I vote that we give the *turista* one share of stock in the corporation."

I am seconded by Luis Gonzalez, who adds, "One share from the two held by Jesús Rinaldo."

"No!" cries Jesús Rinaldo.

"*Bueno!*" say the others.

"Carried!" says Luis. With a gentle movement, he takes one piece of paper from Jesús Rinaldo's shirt pocket. "Here you are, señor," he smiles. "You are now a stockholder in The Pico Street Transportation Company."

Since he is a beginner, we explain to him how we are organized. The gringo stares at the piece of funny paper. He is like a man with his first tortilla. Suddenly he begins to laugh.

"Lord, oh, Lord!" he cries. "Wait till I show this to my attorneys!" He takes a card from his billfold. "Marie," he says to the señora, "this is probably the best investment I ever made."

"You will not regret it, señor," I reply, taking the card. "We will send you every month your share of the profits from our corporation."

"Señor President," the *turista* answers with a fine smile, "this share of stock will be more than enough. Keep my share of the profits and plow it back into the corporation. Take it as a gift."

He is a generous man, this gringo. I thank him for all. In a little while, when we have said our names around, he and the fine señora take a last look at the trailer and slide off in the fat car with much laughter. As they go, it occurs to me that, in a way, as president, I am entitled to three pieces of profits in the corporation. A small thought, but a good one.

When Sam Hondo demands that somebody fork over one buck for fixing the tire, I pay him from my own pocket.

Luis Gonzalez sits with a worried look, staring at his piece of funny paper. "I still do not like this matter of owning things," he says sadly. "Someday I will forget and roll a cigarette with this thing."

"What would you rather have?" I ask carefully.

"A good friend," he answers. "One I can borrow from sometimes. One who will remember me when I am gone."

"I am that friend," I answer soberly.

When he hands me the share of stock, much happiness shines in his eyes. "Now," he says, "I am a rich man, and can still go through the eye of the needle."

Rosita's father whispers me outside as he leaves. "Paco," he says, "you behaved well just now, and with good sense. I am going to give my share of stock to Rosita, and may it bring happiness to you both." He is a good man, Señor Santee, and I say in my heart that someday soon I will be a good son to him.

There is much talk in the shop now, but it adds up only to the fact that I will take boards and fix the trailer. When that is done, it will remain to be ironed out what I am to receive for my work before the profits.

When I tell Rosita, she is overjoyed. "Five shares of profits, and your salary already!" she cries. And then she advises
a wise thing. "Take a long time to get the shine wagon ready,"
she whispers. "Do not move too fast. We can afford to wait
a little longer."

My Rosita is as smart as she is beautiful. Before the week
is out, Jesús Rinaldo has been cleaned at the laundry, playing poker, and I have bought his share of stock for ten dollars.
José Gonzalez comes wanting a loan to buy a new lawn
mower, and in the end sells me his share for ten dollars also.
Señor La Paz, who has never had faith in his piece of paper
from the start, is willing to sell for eight dollars. Still there
are no profits and I let it be known that there are many delays
in arranging my city permit to do business. Rosita lends me
a little, with the understanding it is only a loan to be paid
back, and in a month I have picked up all the stock but two
shares.

My cousin Manuel each day has become more stubborn,
and will not part with his two shares for any amount I can
offer. But he knows, too, that I can put off starting the
business forever. He is only a small minority, and could be
voted out of his treasurer job any time. Yet he counts on my
great love for Rosita, and in the end he knows he will win.

It is true. A night comes when my Rosita and I decide we
can wait no longer. And after all, I consider, Manuel is my
cousin. Outside of business, I have much affection for him.
So the day of our marriage is decided, and it is necessary for
me to begin the business. Such work I have not known before,
but it is like panning gold.

On the Saturday night of my first week, I sit down with
Manuel at the table and we face the problem of dividing his
share after my labor and expenses. The counting is very hard
because we are unhappy. He looks at me a long time and
finally he smiles a slow, tight smile.

"It will not be necessary," he says. His eyes return to the
money before us as if there were nothing more beautiful.

Quickly he pushes me two pieces of funny paper across the table, and there is a hot cherry of fire on his cigar as he speaks around it.

"A little wedding present," he says, "from the stingiest *hombre* on earth."

In my mind I promise that my cousin Manuel will never want for good cigars as long as he lives. And I know, when I have told Rosita, that she will embrace him too. At our table there will always be a place for him, and besides, he still has the chairs and awning.

There is but one thing that is not right, and I speak it to Rosita on the day of our marriage.

"I feel I have been hard in business with my friends," I confess. "I must find a way to make it up to them."

My Rosita is all smiles as she kisses me. "I will feed them my best cooking," she whispers, "and they will make the best baby sitters on all Pico Street. *Mi bien*, you will see."

THE BEAUTIFUL BICYCLE

It is after breakfast and my uncle, Luis Gonzalez, sits with his feet on the table. He is picking the halibut from his teeth with a split match. My father, José, has spread out a handful of cigarette butts from the tin can and is hunting for the brand he likes. There is wine in the gallon bottle, and a sweet smell of eucalyptus comes from the stove.

"Patience, Pedro!" My Uncle Luis speaks with disapproval. He is watching me from between sleepy eyes. "You should not work your toes against the floor. She is a bad habit."

He has warned me of this impatience before.

"I have won many hands of poker," he informs me, "because I can feel a man's toes grabbing at nothing under a table." He makes a sound in his back tooth that is like lifting the air hose from a valve stem. "Something is eating on you," he says to me. "I know. A person who wiggles his toes is hiding something. You have hardly said two words since you got up."

"Leave him alone, Luis," my father says gently. "It is natural sometimes not to talk."

My father is a very quiet man. Before my mamma ran off with the lettuce picker from Imperial Valley she used to say if he did not talk sometimes she would scream. Now he has found a cigarette he likes. He pours more coffee for us both and lights the cigarette from a small twig of cedar which he holds in the stove. Cedar is good for the lungs, he says. He keeps a small bundle of these twigs under the stove. They are from the deodar cedar. Whenever he cuts a lawn where there is such a tree in the yard, he brings home a few twigs.

Uncle Luis has not taken his eyes from my face. "Sometimes I feel this boy does not trust us," he complains.

"Is there a reason he should be so simple?" my father inquires.

Maybe he is remembering all the times my Uncle Luis has gone through my pants pockets in the dark. He gives me a small wink over his coffee cup.

Because I am nervous I pick louder on the wire spokes of the old bicycle wheel in my lap. It is a front wheel which I found in the city dump of Santa Monica. I would not take anything in the world for this wheel. It is part of something wonderful that I think about all the time. But I would not dare to let my Uncle Luis know about this for anything. I must not tell my father, either, but for a different reason.

"Either you have something which belongs to another," Uncle Luis says now, "or you want something you shouldn't. Otherwise, you would not be so jumpy."

In my Uncle Luis' book there is nothing worse than owning things. He often apologizes for his guitar when it is not in the hock shop, and for the small grappling hook on a rope which he uses to fish salvage from the Santa Monica pier. It is because of this hook that he is known everywhere as The Gonzalez Salvage Company. Property is a vanity, he says; the less one has in this world the better off one is. He often repeats this to people who have dropped things from the pier. If they believe him and leave what has fallen into the water, he fishes it out later and sells it on the open market. The open market is in Los Angeles, and my Uncle Luis does not like to talk about it.

My father is sipping his coffee. He follows my fingers along the wire spokes and there is the same sadness in his face as when he watches my Uncle Luis play the guitar. "It is not so bad to want something," he says softly. "I have wanted a lawn mower for many years and it has not hurt me."

Since my father can only cut lawns where people furnish their own machines, he does not have many jobs. It is Uncle Luis who has persuaded him it is better not to work so much than to have a big investment in machinery. But my father often speaks of the lawn mower with regret, and a few times he has had almost enough money to buy one.

My father stirs in his chair. He rubs on the windowpane to see if it is a real fog outside. "The sun will be nice and hot by eleven o'clock," he says. "Perhaps we can go to the pier."

I see he is trying to pull the talk away from me, but it is no use.

"There was a man once who found a hub cap," Uncle Luis says to the ceiling. "Pretty soon this man had to have a wheel. Presently only a whole automobile would satisfy him. It was the worst thing that could have happened to him. The day he got the automobile they put him in jail, and he has been there ever since. It is something to remember, Pedro, if you ever find a hub cap." He fastens his eyes on my bicycle wheel as if it is the stolen automobile and I have been caught red-handed.

My father laughs. "The last time you told that story she was a hairpin that was found," he points out.

"It is only the principle that is important," Uncle Luis replies. "All mistakes are made with an innocent beginning."

Suddenly I find I have made an impolite hiccup. "Pardon!" I say quickly.

"This morning you must ask Señora Cerrito at the grocery store to give you some baking soda," my father says. "She is very good for the stomach."

"In all his life I have never heard this boy burp before," Uncle Luis says with suspicion. "Only an uneasy mind makes such a noise after eating."

"I want to get my work done," I say, to change the subject.

Before I can sweep out and wash the dishes, my father and Uncle Luis must be made to move. It is the same every morning, and it is a matter of feeling. A day can be destroyed, they say, if it is hurried at the beginning.

My father stands looking into the piece of mirror on the wall and decides it is no use shaving until Sunday. My Uncle Luis points to the calendar which is behind the stove. On it are marked all the saints' days. It is because of this calendar that many people say there is a good streak in my Uncle Luis after all.

"What day is she today?" he asks.

"August eleventh. Saint Susanna's day," I reply. Since he asks this same question every morning, I have already looked.

"That one, she's a pretty one!" he says. Now he will tell everybody he meets today it is Saint Susanna's day. He scratches himself around the ribs and takes a comic book from the box by the door. "She's a fine day for feeling good!" he yawns. He stretches himself until he is sure everything is working. It is a funny thing but my Uncle Luis always feels better when the saint's day is a woman. A woman has a better understanding of sin, he says.

When Uncle Luis has gone out on the porch, my father comes to me and rubs my hair with his hand. On his finger is the blue turquoise ring which was given him by my mother. The silver band is heavy and I can feel it through my hair as he pats me. This ring has never been off his finger. It is a beautiful thing and like an extra knuckle on the fist in a fight. He has sworn to my Uncle Luis that if it is ever stolen from his finger while he is drunk, he will kill somebody.

"If I had the money," he says, "I would buy you the most magnificent bicycle on all Pico Street,"

"Then you know what I want?" I cry.

"Of course," he answers. "One cannot help knowing."

"And Uncle Luis—do you think he knows too?" I ask. My heart is pounding, because if Uncle Luis knows I will never be able to get a bicycle. It will be like my father's lawn mower.

"Luis knows it too," he answers sadly.

"I want a bicycle more than anything!" I cry. "With a bicycle I can get a paper route and make much money. I have been promised. I can deliver packages for people. When we catch fish I can hang them from the handle bars and sell them."

Because it would make my father unhappy, I do not tell him of all the other boys in school who have bicycles. When school starts again I would like to ride with them. I can see myself sailing down Pico Street hill ahead of everybody.

"Besides," I point out, "I will not wear out my school shoes if I have a bicycle. It will be a saving there."

"True," my father sighs, "but you do not have the shoes either." He looks at my bare feet. "You must have a pair before school starts," he says. "If a man has good shoes and a good hat, he is never pitied. You must remember that." He rubs my head some more. "Perhaps something will turn up," he says. "Perhaps there will be one on the punch board in Manuel Velez's barbershop someday and we can win it. One must not lose hope."

My father does not beat my ears down when I want something, the way my Uncle Luis does, but he does not help much either. The thing I must be careful about is not to make him sad because he is not rich.

"I might break my neck on a lousy bicycle," I say. "The traffic is very bad. Besides, I would need a license. And Uncle Luis might sell it to buy wine anyway." I steal a look at my father to see if he believes all this. "Only a crazy kid would want a bicycle!" I say with scorn.

"To be happy, sometimes one must also be crazy," he answers. He has lifted the wine bottle from the table, but now he puts it down without drinking. "I think I have a lawn to cut someplace," he says. "If anybody should ask for me, say I will be back presently." It is a thing my father always says when he goes out, but nobody has ever asked for him.

When he is gone, my Uncle Luis shouts for me to come out on the porch. "So you want a bicycle?" he asks. He has heard us talking inside, and there is nothing one can do. "So you think you can make money with a bicycle, it that it?" he demands.

He is asking this to trick me, maybe, but I explain to him how many boys have paper routes and how much they are paid for each paper delivered.

"The world is full of bicycles," he answers. "I should think you could borrow one."

"Who would lend me his bicycle?" I demand with scorn. "It is only by begging that I have even learned to ride one. I want my own!"

"A bicycle is an insignificant piece of property," he says. Then he adds in a low voice to his toes, "But so is a hen which lays eggs every day. Have you saved any money to get this bicycle?"

"No."

"And so far you have only the front wheel of a bicycle?"

"I am looking everywhere for pieces," I explain. "My friends are saving any which turn up. Every day I go to the city dump. Sometime I might even find a whole bicycle." I do not tell him that already I have found two tires, a chain and a front mudguard which I am keeping at Sam Hondo's garage. Sam has promised to help me build the bicycle when I have collected all the parts. I am afraid if my Uncle Luis knew about these parts he would want to sell them on the open market.

"I have many connections," he says grandly. "I will look into this matter of a bicycle and see what is best for us."

"It would be better if you forgot all about my bicycle," I say with worry. "Perhaps I would only get into trouble with a bicycle anyway."

He pretends he does not hear me. His eyes are closed and his hands are folded across his stomach. He will not move for two hours, I think.

But when I have washed the dishes and am sweeping out through the front door, I see he is gone. His grappling hook, which was beside the geranium can on the porch, is also missing, so I know he has gone to the pier. When I have finished my housework I start out up Pico Street, rolling my front wheel before me.

Remembering what my father has said, I stop at the grocery store to see Señora Cerrito. "Today is Saint Susanna's day!" I say, and stand before the meat case with my tongue hanging out. When she gives me a nice piece of salami she asks where is my lazy father and my no-good uncle these days, so I have to say they are working hard. "They are going to get me a bicycle before school starts," I say, to make talk.

"I can just see it!" Señora Cerrito laughs. "Any bicycle you get from them you will ride in your sleep. It will be a dream." She puts crackers into my pocket and boots me from her store. She is a very nice woman.

At the barbership Manuel Velez is standing with the comb behind his ear, and my father is sitting along the wall with Jesús Rinaldo, the gambler. They are listening to Manuel's radio, and my father is talking into Jesús Rinaldo's ear. He has forgotten about the lawn he was going to cut.

I go through many alleys and when I reach the city dump I look over everything which is new since yesterday. There is not one lousy piece of bicycle. When the whistles blow for lunchtime, it works out that I am just coming into the front door of Sam Hondo's garage.

He is opening the big lunch box which his wife, Rosa, fixes for him every day. He hands me a chicken enchilada.

"Any luck today?" he asks.

"No," I reply. "People do not throw away bicycle pieces. All the pieces are in the junk yards where they cost money."

"Too bad," he says. When he has given me half his orange, he says, "Look behind that paper carton on the bench. You might find something."

My heart leaps. Since Sam and Rosa do not have any children yet, they sometimes say they would like a boy like me. In the past Rosa has bought me a T shirt and once a sweater, and Sam has given me a pocket knife and a watch which would run if it had not been dropped.

"Go ahead and look," he says.

"A pair of handle bars!" I shout, when I see what it is. I cannot keep from running in a big circle while I hold them in front of me to try them out.

Sam laughs at me being crazy. "I put on a new pair for a guy this morning," he explains. "He left me the old ones for nothing. It was a piece of luck for us."

"Gee, Sam," I say, when I have helped him eat his banana-coconut cake, "do you think I'll ever get a real whole bike?"

"It may take a while," he says. "We'll just have to keep our eyes open."

"If I could only get it before school starts!"

"I know," he nods. "You could make a little money to help out at home. You could ride with the kids."

When I have put the handle bars with the other pieces and am rolling my wheel home past Manuel Velez's barbershop, I see that my father is gone. Manuel grabs me by the pants and wants to know where is the rest of my bicycle. He tells me he has seen a man in a circus who could ride on only one wheel. He is a person to tease people and I have to put up with him.

"Did you see the bicycle riders go by on their way to the pier?" he asks. "A lot of rich gringos from Beverly Hills. It was a club. You never saw such bicycles in your life."

"When?" I cry. I must have missed them because I was in Sam Hondo's garage.

"A couple of hours ago," Manuel replies. "They looked like monkeys hung up by the back on a wash line. Such racing bicycles are very uncomfortable."

"Racing bikes!" I cry. "Maybe they are still on the pier!"

I take off with all my might down Pico Street to see if maybe I can get to the pier in time. There are bicycle racks along the railings near the café. If I am in time I will see some terrific bikes, and I will try to talk to the men who own them. But when I have crossed the overpass to the pier I know it is no use. There are no racing bicycles. And when I have looked around the pier I cannot even find my Uncle Luis. At the bait house I learn that they have seen him, but it was hours ago.

"He's here when the bike she'sa get lost," Mr. Pasquales says. "The police he'sa grab Luis, but for why? He'sa no got it. So he's don't got took in. Too bad!"

I learn from others at the Harbor Office that one of the rich gringo riders has lost his bicycle while everybody was eating in the café. It is something which nobody can understand. The pier has been searched underneath, but there is no sign of the bicycle. Everybody is still laughing at the gringo, who had to go home in a taxi.

Since a bicycle is too big to be put into a sack and carried away, my Uncle Luis is innocent for once. I say a big thanks to Saint Susanna who has kept him from trouble. But I am still full of worry because my Uncle Luis is a man to see everything. If he did not make the bicycle disappear, it is a cinch he has seen something to make himself disappear. I think I had better get home to see if he is there.

When I come into the house it is very empty. My father and Uncle Luis are not there. Because it is lonesome, I start a fire in the stove and sit down to wait. I cannot take my mind from the expensive bicycle which is lost. If the police have got my Uncle Luis again, I do not even know where I can find my father to tell him. There is nothing he can do, but he should know anyway.

I am afraid to leave because I think they might come home any minute. But when it is dark and I am hungry, I consider that Carmelita Smith at the Caliente Café will give me a candy bar if I go there. Since she is a person to kiss me sometimes, I think the least I can do is to wash my face.

I have but put my face in the pan when there is a step on the porch and my Uncle Luis stands in the door. He is holding a great granddaddy lobster on the grappling hook and he is full of happiness. He is also with wine, I think. His hat is gone and he is wearing seaweed around his head.

"Put the pan on the stove," he says. "First we will boil the lobster. You can wash any time."

Since lobster is out of season, I tell him he is very lucky some policeman is not going to eat it for him. "Did you scratch him up with the hook?" I ask.

"It is a long story," he says, laughing. When he flops on the bed I know he will not move until we have eaten the lobster. "Saint Susanna is a beautiful woman," he says presently. "The water was very dirty. Pedro, my nephew, you must be very good to your Uncle Luis all your life. There is nothing he would not do for you."

"What do you mean?" I demand.

"It was an old man," he says. "An old man who was trying to kill himself with so much exercise. If I had not come like an instrument of heaven, he would have been dead before he got back to where he started. But with a little pull on the blessed hook, I saved his life."

He is talking crazy. "You better sleep it off," I say. "You are boiled worse than this lobster."

"Look under the porch," he says, as if he is a great magician. "You will see something to prove I am the best uncle you ever had."

Since anything can be under the porch, I think I had better look. Outside, I peep into the dark hole.

My heart stops. It is a bicycle. It is such a bicycle as I have never seen before. There is much seaweed on it and the water drips from the joints, but it shines and sparkles until I am afraid to touch it.

All at once I think I am going to be sick. It is the racing bike that was lost from the pier. My Uncle Luis has stolen it! If they catch him now, they will salt him down until the Resurrection Day. It is all I can do to go back inside. He has done a generous thing, but he does not understand that such a bicycle is impossible.

When I try to speak, I can only stand by the bed and shake my head. I cannot open my mouth.

My Uncle Luis regards me with much affection. "A little jerk with the hook and she fell into the sea," he says. "When it was dark, I fished her out again. There was even a lobster caught in the spokes of the wheel. What more could one ask?"

"They—they'll murder you for this!" I burst out.

"It is all thought through," he replies. "We will take this bicycle apart very carefully. We will trade the pieces for other pieces on the open market. We will take our time. Presently you will have another bicycle which cannot be recognized. Then you can have the paper route and pay back poor old Uncle Luis for all his trouble. In the meantime we have saved an old man's life and had lobster besides for supper." He shuts his eyes and blows out his lips with a deep breath. "Wake me up when she is ready," he says.

I think my Uncle Luis is right. If we traded the pieces for other pieces, we would never be caught. But how could I explain these pieces to my good friend Sam Hondo? And what if the police found my Uncle Luis in the open market? What is worse, it would still be a stolen bicycle. I would be ashamed to ride it to school. Whenever somebody looked at me my toes would be grabbing in my shoes. I would be guilty.

When the lobster is boiled, my father still has not come home. Uncle Luis has his head under the pillow so he can sleep better. I am starving to eat the lobster, and I am remembering that Father Lomita, the priest, has often said that he doubts my Uncle Luis' influence on me is for the best. When I can stand it no longer, I break off a small claw and run outside. I crack the claw with my teeth and the meat is sweet and warm.

As I look up into the sky I know I must take the bicycle back. If I do it before my father comes home, he will not be sad because he must make me do it. He will not have to argue all night with Uncle Luis. We can eat the lobster in peace.

When I pull the bike from beneath the porch and spin the wheels, I listen to see how much sand is in the axles. But it is not bad. The grease has kept the sand and water out. I think it will not hurt things too much if I ride it. It will be only once. And not far, only to the pier.

It is light as a feather. I have never been on such a light bike. And the faster I go the less chance I have of being caught. My legs sing with joy and my feet press the pedals faster and faster. When I hit the overpass to the pier I think I am going to take off like a sea gull. I am already gritting my teeth to think I must ever get off of such a wonderful thing.

Then it is all over. I spin through the row of lights and into the shadow beside the Harbor Office. There are still people on the pier and I am afraid I have been seen by somebody who knows I have no business on such a bike. In another second I have left it where it will be found and have slipped down the ladder beside the oil dock.

I know the crosspieces under the pier as well as my Uncle Luis. I find my way in the dark on the planks by the sewer line all the way down to the fish company and come up by another ladder. I am safe now, and nobody will ever know. The man will soon have his bicycle back. But what will I tell my Uncle Luis?

When I open the door very softly my Uncle Luis shouts to me that it is about time I showed up. He is sitting at the table with the hot lobster before him.

"I thought you went to find Papa José!" he scolds me. "Where does he think he is all day?"

"He was with Jesús Rinaldo this morning," I say.

"Sit down," he tells me. "Maybe he has been invited out to dinner. Jesús Rinaldo has been winning lately and he is not one to keep his money."

"Uncle Luis—" I begin.

"There is a side claw missing from this lobster," he says with disapproval. "It is a greedy little boy who does not have patience to wait until mealtime."

"I took back the bicycle you stole," I burst out. "I left it outside the Harbor Office, where they will find it. You are a very good uncle to get it for me, but I do not want you to go to jail. It would not be right to ride a stolen bicycle to school and the church and every place."

"Ingratitude!" It is a heavy word from Uncle Luis' lips. He regards me with much sorrow.

"You have destroyed my whole day's work," he says gloomily. "It is a thankless business to try to help people. Now you will have no paper route and you will have to walk when others ride. But for one thing I am happy."

"What?" I demand miserably.

"You have had the courage not to desire an insignificant piece of property. A boy with a paper route would be worse off than a man with a cow that has to be milked twice a day. You would have been a slave to the system."

"But I want a bicycle!" I cry. "I want a paper route!" My throat is tight, as if I am choking, and I want to hammer my Uncle Luis on the head because he does not understand. "Can't you see? If you just hadn't stolen it, you big — big —"

"We will eat the lobster," he says. "She is big enough for four people. When your stomach is full, you will not want everything so much." He lifts the long knife and splits the lobster. "Wipe your nose," he grumbles.

"I — I don't want any," I answer, and hide my face in my arms.

Uncle Luis is cracking the lobster and making sounds as if he is in a bad accident. Suddenly there is a great noise on the porch and my father bangs through the door with a great clatter.

"Pedro!" he shouts. "My little Pedro! What do you think of this?"

He is standing in the middle of the floor, and beside him is a bicycle. I cannot move. It is not a new bicycle, but it has a luggage rack and a light on the handle bars, and it has fine tires with lots of tread.

"If I could ride this thing I would have been here sooner," my father pants. "I pushed it all the way from West Hollywood."

That is ten miles. My father has pushed this bicycle ten miles. Still I cannot speak. If he has taken this bicycle from somebody without paying, I think I will die.

"Come here, boy," he says. "I am tired holding it. My feet are killing me."

I am like walking in my sleep when I touch it. It has rubber handle grips, and rubber pedals, and a double-built fork.

"Who—whose is it?" I whisper.

"For you, Pedro," my father says. "For who else would I walk so far?" He sits at the table. He takes off his shoes. He sees the lobster and smiles at my Uncle Luis. "Saint Susanna, she's good to you today, huh, Luis?"

My Uncle Luis nods. He cannot take his eyes from me and from the bicycle. "She is not so good as the racing type," he says. "But not bad for you, José. Not bad at all! Are you sure you have not been followed?"

My father smiles a big smile. "There is nothing to worry about," he says. He takes a paper from his pocket and holds it with great tenderness. "She is all here on the paper."

I know then that he has not stolen it. "Papa! Papa!" I lay down the bicycle and run to him. My arms are around his neck. "You are the best man in the whole world!" And I hug him until he has to cough to get more breath.

"It took money," my Uncle Luis says with suspicion. "How did we get this money?"

"Not much," my father explains. "Manuel Velez knew of this bicycle through his sister who works in the beauty parlor on Hollywood Boulevard. A woman who comes there has a son in the Army who has written to her to sell his bicycle because now he has only one leg." My father stops, shaking his head because it is a sad thought.

"And so?" Uncle Luis inquires.

"So I got eight dollars from Jesús Rinaldo and went to Manuel's sister and then to the woman." My father stares at the floor. "It was very hard. We are very fortunate to have nobody fighting in the Army. She let me have the bicycle for eight dollars.. There are twenty-two dollars yet to pay. It will be a dollar a week for twenty-two weeks. It is all here on the paper."

"Then we are in debt," my Uncle Luis says heavily.

"With the paper route, Pedro will be able to pay it," my father replies. "I will always have lawns to cut."

"I will be able to make that much every day!" I cry. "It will be nothing! You will see what a big thing a paper route is!"

"And you will be able to ride to school," my father says softly. "You will be able to go with the other boys."

My Uncle Luis does not look happy. "So you got eight dollars from Jesús Rinaldo?" he says.

"Yes," my father replies, but it is plain he does not wish to speak more about it. "Tell me how you got the lobster, Luis," he says. "It was a long trip and I am starved."

When we sit at the table Uncle Luis slides his foot on top of mine and begins a long story of how he brought up the granddaddy lobster on his hook from under the pier. "I had an old fish head on the hook for bait," he says. "This foolish animal could not resist it."

I see he does not want my father to learn about the trouble with the racing bicycle. Because I am sure he did not mean to do a bad thing, I stuff my mouth with lobster and keep still. It would only make my father nervous anyway.

The lobster is so good and the bicycle is so beautiful I think I have never been so happy in my whole life. And then all at once I am sad. I remember Sam Hondo and how hard we have worked to get pieces for the bicycle he was going to help me build. But I cannot speak of this. When my father and Uncle Luis are not looking, I take a nice piece of lobster from the shell and hide it in my lap. Tomorrow I will take it to Sam for his lunch. I know he will be glad for me about my new bicycle because he is my good friend.

Suddenly I see my Uncle Luis is not eating. My father, too, has stopped, his hand halfway to his mouth. He is holding a small lobster claw.

"Only eight dollars?" my Uncle Luis asks.

My father lays down the lobster claw and puts his hand beneath the table. All at once I understand.

"Papa! Your ring!" I cry.

My father takes a big breath and smiles. "I have often told Jesús Rinaldo it was a lucky ring," he says. "He has wanted to buy it for a long time. Do not trouble yourself about it. It was nothing."

But I know and Uncle Luis knows, and a great silence falls upon us. It was my mother's ring. It was the only thing my father ever had that he would fight anybody to keep. Now he has sold it to Jesús Rinaldo for eight dollars to buy me a bicycle.

"A bicycle is better than a ring," he says. "Just as the future is better than the past."

My Uncle Luis pours wine into the cup for my father and hunts in the can for a cigarette, which he passes across the table.

"We will get the ring back, José" he says softly. "If Rinaldo should give it to a woman, I will get it from her if it takes every string on my guitar to do it."

"We will speak no more of it," my father answers. He stands at the stove, lighting the cigarette with a twig. He is very thin and tall, and his shoulders are very straight as he blows the smoke in a soft cloud before him.

As I touch my bicycle I say a promise in my heart to Saint Susanna. I will get my father's ring back for him even if it takes all my life. I will deliver more papers than anybody in the world.

"Look!" I cry. "Look, papa!" And when I have put a chair to steady me, I sit on the bicycle and pretend I am riding ahead of everybody.

INVENTION OF THE DEVIL

What my mother does not know is that my sister Blanquita is often seen on Juanito Retaco's motorcycle. If she knew it, her hair would turn white.

"It is an invention of the devil," she says now. Her apron is full of pea hulls which she throws over the fence to the chickens. "A girl in her right mind would have nothing to do with a man who rides one," she argues. "The world is full of widows who married men on motorcycles."

Blanquita flops herself over on the blanket where she is tanning herself to look like a movie star.

"When you married Pete Escobar he was riding a handcar," she points out.

"But not for long," my mother says grimly. She stands at the screen door. She shakes her head over Blanquita. "Was lousy idea," she sighs. "A man on wheels is a headache to everybody." She goes into the house.

Before Blanquita was born, my father worked on the Southern Pacific. He rode a handcar every day. Wine and handcars do not mix. Now he works close to home for the Pacific Electric. He walks the tracks in a red jacket, with a big wrench, a broom and a bucket of grease. Everybody knows Pete Escobar. He is the only man on Pico Street who can play a zither. If it were not for Blanquita, he would get a good night's sleep for a change.

"She has imagination," he often says He means she is always in some kind of trouble. She is never satisfied until a thing is made different.

At the Granada picture show where she operates a flashlight, it is understood she is helping them out only until her movie contract comes through. Or until she enters a convent. Or until she is disinherited by her family for working, since no woman of the Escobars has ever worked before.

"She is that age," my mother often sighs. "First is with rabbits and snakes in cages. Now is a man on a motorcycle."

Because it is school vacation, my sister has an idea with frying herself in the sun. She is expecting Juanito to come by. "The morning is half gone!" she complains.

"Don't hold your breath," I tell her. I am turning my bike upside down on the walk to oil the coaster brake. "Maybe he is dead in a ditch."

She looks at me as if I am unnecessary.

The old one, my grandfather, is on a bench where he can smell the peach tree. His manzanita stick is between his knees, and his eyes are shut to the warm sun. He opens them a crack to look at the blossoms.

"It is a day to make one glad he did not die last week," he says sleepily. "Who is dead in a ditch?"

"Nobody," I tell him. "But it could be Juanito Retaco."

"Impossible," he objects. "Señor Retaco is a fine horseman. He rode all the way from Sonora. He has seen the Gulf of California."

"Not him," I explain. "It's his grandson, Juanito. The one who is going to the University of California at Los Angeles."

"The one with the motorcycle," Blanquita says. "The handsome one."

My grandfather shudders. He knows now who is meant. "He should be working," he mutters. "He should not be allowed loose to destroy a morning."

Because the university is on vacation, Juanito is resting his head from the books. My father says he could get Juanito a job on the track crew with the Pacific Electric. Blanquita says who does he think Juanito is to be a common laborer? My mother replies he could do worse, and maybe will before he is through. There has been much argument. The truth is that

Juanito's father owns a small piece of land which he leases for truck farming. Juanito rides twelve miles to the university on a chrome-job motorcycle with silver-mounted saddlebags. Foxtails fly from each grip of the handle bars. He does not need a job. He is going to be a lawyer someday.

When we hear him blasting his exhaust three blocks away, Blanquita combs her hair and fixes her lips. She stretches out limp as a hot possum, to play dead. When Juanito slides into the drive on one wheel, the dust piles up like smoke from an oil fire. He kills the engine. He leaps from the saddle.

"Blanquita!" he cries. "How's for a quick run up to Santa Barbara?"

Santa Barbara is ninety miles. He does it there and back in two hours. But he is dreaming. My mother already stands at the back door.

"No rides!" she screams in alarm. "You hear, Blanquita? Blanquita!"

But Blanquita is like she has swallowed sleeping pills. She is a slumbering princess . . . she thinks.

"Mamma Escobar!" Juanito shouts. "I will take you too!"

"You take nobody!" she says.

Juanito is wearing his leather kidney belt studded with rubies. His overalls are rolled up from his black boots. He is shining in the sun like a slim pistol.

When he throws himself beside Blanquita, my mother hurries into the yard. Blanquita raises on one elbow and gives her a look to scare baby-sitters. It is no use. My mother is already on the bench with potatoes to peel.

"That motorcycle stinks like a goat," she says. "I should think you would get rid of it."

"It's only a clean gasoline smell."

"Is the odor of Satan," she says.

"Oh, for goodness sake, mamma!" Blanquita cries. "Please let me go for a ride with Juanito."

"No."

Blanquita turns on Juanito. "I told you," she sighs. "There is no use asking some people." Her chin quivers as if she is going to cry.

"About the fiesta Saturday night," Juanito asks. "Are we going?"

Blanquita has already asked my mother. It was what started the whole argument about Juanito and men who ride motorcycles. She had been thumbsdown on the idea. Now I can see that she is sorry for Blanquita. She is trying to think if there is any harm in the fiesta.

"We are all going," she says finally. "One more will make no difference."

Suddenly Juanito is on his feet. "Señor Escobar!" He bows to my grandfather in respect.

The old one has come up behind us and stands leaning on his stick. He asks to be remembered to Juanito's parents. "Have you seen our peach tree?" he asks.

"It's beautiful," Juanito replies.

"Do you know the story of the tree?" the old one inquires.

"No," Juanito replies.

"Tell him," my grandfather instructs my mother.

It is a story my mother loves. She relates to Juanito how the peach tree was planted on the day Blanquita was born. She watched my father through a bedroom window as he dug a hole and put in the little switch. My grandfather carried water and helped. "When the first peach came," she finishes with much tenderness, "it was given to Blanquita to eat all by herself."

Juanito has been staring at the peach tree and at the pink blossoms underneath on the ground. Now he looks at Blanquita as if she is more wonderful then ten peach trees.

"I understand," he says. "It's the same way with me. At home they treat me as if I am going to be the future governor. They hate my motorcycle."

"Still they permit you to ride it," my mother says severely.

It is Blanquita who snaps back at my mother. "If somebody wants something all his life," she demands, "why shouldn't he have it?"

When Juanito climbs on his machine to leave, Blanquita stands picking hairs from the foxtails on the handle grip. He guns the motor at everything she is saying. My mother's apron flies out. The pink under the peach tree goes up in a cloud. By the time he has roared away, even the grass lies flat as fish scales. The old one has gone in the shed and shut the door.

My mother looks down at me and at the pieces of bike I have spread out. "Wheels!" she says in disgust. "Men and their wheels!" She has the screen door in her hand when Blanquita raises a cry to heaven.

"Mamma! What will I wear to the fiesta?"

"Wear what you got," my mother answers.

"I must have a new dress."

"There is no money."

"You don't want me to have a new dress!" Blanquita howls. "You don't want me to go with Juanito! You never want me to have any fun!"

My mother says firmly, "Come here, Blanquita. Some ways you are grown up. Some ways you are still six years old. While we make a batch of enchiladas we will talk about it."

Blanquita's lips are tight shut but she picks up her blanket and follows my mother inside.

My father is not like my mother. Usually he is not a man to worry over small things. From the tracks he has observed Juanito and Blanquita many times on the highway. He has tried to forget it. But tonight when he comes home he is very serious. When we have had our supper he sits picking his zither with a bad rhythm. All at once he spreads his big hands on the strings as if he is tearing dead hairs from a hairbrush.

"That Juanito!" he groans. "This morning he missed the P. E. train at the crossing only by the thickness of a tortilla. Someday we will be picking him up in a bucket."

"You hear, Blanquita?" my mother cries.

"He was going to Santa Barbara," I put in. "He was mad."

Blanquita looks up from the table where she and my mother have been arguing over a dress pattern. Her face has become a little pale.

"But he missed it!" she cries proudly. "He always does!"

"So far," my father says angrily. "But someday he will wind up where he won't scare the hell out of people." He looks hard at Blanquita. "Sooner than you think," he predicts.

"I am going to have a plunging neckline," Blanquita announces quickly, "or nothing at all." She is pulling the talk another way.

"Why another dress?" my father demands.

"For the fiesta," my mother replies. "Blanquita is going with the crazy one who cannot live without a motorcycle."

"Please, papa!" Blanquita runs to him. "Why can't I have a new dress?"

"No money," my mother says firmly.

My father sighs. "Sure," he says softly, "why not?" When he puts his hands under Blanquita's chin, it is like he is lifting a camellia against his cheek. He is already seeing her in a new dress. He is sad because she is in love with Juanito who will kill himself one day. He is happy because she will be the prettiest girl at the fiesta.

"No bought dress!" my mother says flatly.

"We will think about it," my father replies.

Blanquita puts her head against his knee. "The fiesta is only a few days away," she sighs. "I want you to be proud of me, papa."

"Sure," he nods.

My mother stands with her hands on both hips. "When you think you can manage money better than me, I will give you the bills," she says.

They smile at her. Even my grandfather smiles. It is always a joke that my mother wants to give other people the bills. Nothing is more impossible.

The next evening when he comes home from work, my father is carrying a big bundle in brown paper. "There is an answer to everything," he announces. "Today the finance company has taken back Emilio Garcia's automobile."

"What now?" my mother groans.

"Fifty yards of the finest white silk!" my father exclaims. "It cost the government a fortune." He unrolls the bundle. It is a terrific silk parachute. He shakes it up and it floats out all over the room.

"It has been stolen!" my mother cries.

My father laughs. "Emilio bought it at the surplus store to cover his automobile. He never used it, and now he does not need it."

"So he talks you into it!" my mother snaps.

"Only a few bucks," my father shrugs," and not till payday. Here is silk for everything!"

Blanquita has grabbed an armful of the white silk and is holding it to her. "You are wonderful, papa," Her eyes are big as flashlights. . . . "See, mamma; it will make a full circle skirt. The biggest, most wonderful one in the world." She whirls to show how it will fly out.

"Maybe some panels out first," my mother relents. "Such silk!" She is measuring the big chute with her eyes.

My father climbs out of the middle. He has made a sale. "It is a matter of imagination," he says proudly. "The best dressmakers in Paris are men."

He motions the old one and me to follow him. Blanquita and my mother do not even know we are gone. Outside, we sit on the bench, and my father gives the old one a cigar he has bought for him. "It is always the man who must think how to do a thing," he tells us. Before us the peach tree is a soft pink. He observes it with much satisfaction. "Blanquita is becoming a woman now," he points out. "A little queen. Nothing is too good for her."

"She was on the motorcycle with Juanito again today," I say.

For a second I think my father will slap me. "Shut up," he answers in a dead voice. "I saw them. Until you have to open your big mouth, I had forgotten it."

"Forbid her to ride with him," the old one commands. "Put your foot down!"

But my father shakes his head. "She would only feel more guilty. She would ride anyway." He rubs his knuckles. "She is like me," he frowns. "She thinks nothing can go wrong when one is happy."

"Then is the worst time," the old one replies. He turns his cigar sadly in his thin fingers. "But perhaps you are right. Who is to say what anybody must do?" He is still shaking his head over this when Blanquita comes rushing to us.

"I'm already late for the show!" she cries. "You were super to latch on to the silk chute for me!" She gives my father a big hug.

As he looks after her, there is much love in his face.

In three minutes something goes off like a string of Chinese firecrackers. It is the backfire of a motorcycle down the street.

"*Perdicion!*" my father cries.

The old one pounds the ground with his stick. He is beating Juanito in his mind.

By the next day my father has cooled down. Blanquita and my mother are making the new dress from the parachute. Juanito does not come by, and my grandfather has caught two gophers.

But when the night of the fiesta comes, my sister's blouse is still an argument. My mother has thrown her crimson *rebozo* over Blanquita's shoulders to give modesty to what cannot be helped. The blouse has a plunging neckline which she caught at the last minute with a silver concha. But Blanquita has moved the pin. My father picks at his zither, and we all stand waiting.

"An inch is as bad as a mile!" my mother is storming, when we hear the roar of a motorcycle outside.

In another minute Juanito stands in the door. He is dressed like a rich *caballero* and he is holding out his hat, full of gardenias. He has come to take Blanquita to the fiesta on his motorcycle.

It is an insult to common sense. It is unthinkable. Who are we to permit such a crazy idea?

"Not for a tubful of gardenias!" my mother cries. "Take yourself off! Blanquita will walk with us or she will not go!"

Blanquita is fit to be tied. She wrings her hands. She begs. At last she talks to Juanito alone in the front yard. Finally he roars off by himself.

All the way to St. Ann's, Blanquita does not speak to us. She walks by herself, and we have to follow her like four bad sheep. The old one cannot go fast, and Blanquita gets far ahead. My mother pushes me to catch up with her. Soon we are all separated. It is not a way to come to a fiesta to be happy.

The fiesta, which is given each year in the walled yard of the church, is not for gringos. It is for our own people. The pink-and-white statue of St. Ann herself looks down on the music and dancing. There are strings of lights between the palm and pepper trees. There are booths with games which are played for prizes. The good smell of enchiladas and tacos, coffee and cheese beans comes from the kitchen. In a corner of the wall is a prison of fresh palm branches to which girls wearing police hats and carrying billy clubs take the arrested men who must pay fines for charity. The old ones are on benches along the walls. Small kids are running everywhere at once.

Blanquita swirls through the crowd in her big white skirt. She has found Juanito. When he swings her in his arms, her skirt blooms out like she is a white hibiscus falling from the sky. Everybody has spoken of it. Such a dress was never seen before.

My father is whanging his zither with the musicians. My mother watches from the bench by the wall with the old one.

For a whole hour now Blanquita has been dancing as if she is the hottest dish in California. She is in Juanito's arms like a bundle of love. Her hair is flying, and her lips are parted as if to say he must kiss her or she will die. Everybody is watching them. It is enough to make my mother wild. She ties knots in her fine lace handkerchief. She has not spoken to the Retacos, who are sitting but ten feet from us.

All at once Juanito is holding my sister tight and kissing her. Everywhere there are cheers and shouts. The Retacos are on their feet. My mother screams. My father shoves his zither into the arms of a stranger.

But two of the girls in police caps are there ahead of them. A kiss is a penitentiary offense. They grab Juanito, because it is always the man who is wrong. Blanquita is pleading and making a big fuss. She has got revenge on my mother. But not for long. She has not figured it out far enough. Suddenly she sees Retacos and Escobars coming from all sides.

"Juanito!" she cries in panic. "Break loose! Run!"

She is flying across the yard in a cloud of white.

Juanito tears away from the girls. His hat is snatched off. His shirt is torn from his back. But he is free and is racing after Blanquita. They dodge through the gate to the alley.

"The motorcycle!" I cry to my father. "They are going for Juanito's motorcycle!"

I am heard everywhere. The girl cops shout for the guys who have hot rods to catch the prisoners who are escaping. The whole fiesta has become a crazy place.

"They will be killed!" my mother moans.

The guys are rushing to the alley where the crates are parked. The girls are behind them, crying to be taken.

"Go with them!" my father shouts. He gives me a push that would put my nose in the dirt if I had not already started.

I pile into a cut-down job. "She is my sister!" I shout. Four people are squeezed on top of me.

"They went down Olympic!" somebody cries.

"They'll take the Coast Highway!" another shouts.

We leap after them like a swarm of locusts. When we leave the red light at Santa Monica Canyon, the guy who is driving opens her wide.

We burn the black-top and pray no cop will spot us. We have hit a hundred miles an hour. Suddenly we are shouting, "There they are!"

Ahead of us, taking the new grade behind Malibu Beach, is a single headlight. Behind is a speck of white. At the top of the hill is a great V where the road cuts through, and the light is climbing to it like the spark of a skyrocket.

"Pour it on!" somebody shouts. We hit the bottom of the grade with everything we have.

We are all watching the spark when it disappears. A mushroom of white blows up into the V of the hill. The spark flashes again, high up on one side of the cut. Everybody is struck dumb. The spark has gone out for good.

"She blew off!" somebody gasps.

We are roaring up the grade. My heart has stopped. I am sure Blanquita is killed. Maybe Juanito is dead too. What will become of my father and mother? I am suddenly frozen stiff with terror.

Behind us is the sound of the other cars. We slide in a rain of gravel from the shoulder of the road. We leap from the cars to the side of the cut that slants up to the sky. We stumble to the splash of white lying above us.

When we reach them, my sister is lying in Juanito's arms. She is no more dead than I am. She has her arms around Juanito's neck, and she is holding on to him as if he is the last thing on earth.

The other cars have stopped below us, beaming their lights up. My sister is covered with red clay, and she is a mess.

"You sure fixed yourself this time!" I cry. "You'll never get out of this!" I am so relieved I am shaking mad all over. "You big, crazy dope!" I cry to Juanito.

"Take it easy, Carlos!" Juanito answers. He stands up and speaks only to me. "Your sister is not hurt. We are very lucky."

"It was all my own fault!" Blanquita moans.

Everybody has to know what happened, and Blanquita sobs how she was trying to hold on to Juanito and to her big dress both at once. It swelled up around her into a balloon. It ripped her arms from aroung Juanito's waist and swept her into the soft dirt.

The motorcycle, which hit a boulder in the embankment, still lies with the frame twisted and the headlight buried. Juanito stands rubbing his arm, staring down at the machine.

"Stay with Blanquita," he says. He motions the guys away. "I'll be back in a few minutes." He lifts the cycle from the dirt and rocks. He runs his hands over the broken parts. It is like he is moving a dead thing as he begins pushing her up the side of the cut.

"I'll help you," I say. He does not answer, but I begin to push too. I cannot figure where he is going.

When we reach the top there is a black canyon below us, with the sea beyond. A few lights are along the shore. The wind whips at our faces in the darkness.

He unties the foxtails from the handle bars. Still he has said nothing. His face is set like a hard piece of rock.

"Let go!" he says to me.

With a great push he sends the cycle crashing over the rocks down the side of the canyon. He stands with his fists clenched at his sides. It is a terrible thing. I do not understand what has happened to him.

"That's that!" he says. He motions me to follow him. He does not look back. I cannot understand why he has thrown away so much fine stuff.

When we come to the others, he goes to Blanquita. He takes her hands and gives her one of the foxtails. "Keep it," he says. "Someday we will laugh about tonight."

Something has happened to my sister. She is serious, almost like my mother, as she stands there. The girls have cleaned her up. Her top skirt is off, and she stands in one of the silk underskirts. My mother's crimson *rebozo* still covers her shoulders.

"What will they do to us?" she asks Juanito.

"I don't know," he answers. He curls up the other foxtail and puts it carefully into his pocket. He turns to the others. "How's for a hitch back to the fiesta?" he asks.

"No!" Blanquita objects. "Where is your motorcycle?"

"There is no motorcycle."

"What did you do?" she cries. Suddenly she presses the foxtail against her cheek. All at once she understands.

"Come on," he answers. "Give me your hand."

We are like a funeral procession. It is as if everybody has seen the end of something and nothing will ever be the same again. When we reach St. Ann's the cars creep into the alley.

The girl cops take charge of Juanito and hurry him off to the prison of palm branches. It is there that my father and Señor Retaco go to talk to him. I am waved away.

Blanquita is before my mother and the old one. Señora Retaco is also there.

"Say what happened," my mother commands.

Blanquita tells it all. She does not try to make anything different. There are may gasps of fright as she tells how the wind caught her. The tears are falling from her cheeks as she takes the foxtail from her bosom. She tells how Juanito has destroyed his motorcycle. There will be no more stolen rides. There will be no wild running away again.

"You are a good girl," Señora Retaco says gently.

"Is better now," my mother nods. "Is a strong love now."

"You know I love him?" Blanquita asks in wonder.

"But of course," my mother sighs. "When a peach tree blooms, who can hide it?"

The old one sits without speech. His face is turned to the statue of St. Ann.

My father and Señor Retaco are coming from the prison with Juanito between them. They are talking and smiling.

"Pete," Señor Retaco is advising my father, "what you need on the track crew is a smart young lawyer. One who can pay back his father for a dead motorcycle."

My father beams. Already he can see Juanito working between the rails. It is a thing which has many possibilities. "Sure," he laughs, "why not?" Now he can sleep nights.

Señora Retaco lays a thin hand on my mother's knee. "Only this," she says gently. "The boy must finish his schooling first."

"Blanquita would not have it otherwise," my mother agrees. "How can one be governor of California if one does not study?"

My sister and Juanito can only look at each other. They are lucky to be alive. In their eyes is all the excitement of two foxtails flying in the wind. In their minds they are going faster than on a motorcycle.

A NIGHT TO REMEMBER

It has always been a happy time with us, but this evening my father, who is José Gonzalez, is full of worry, "I do not understand it," he says to my Uncle Luis. "Until now you have stood up as a free man. An example to all. A man who could attend a woman or leave her alone."

"How true!" my Uncle Luis sighs.

"But this Florencia Murphy—" my father groans.

"She is different," Uncle Luis says.

"You think!"

"I know."

"You could be mistaken."

"So she is a woman of experience," Uncle Luis replies. "One does not expect a woman to be perfect."

"But this one! Señora Murphy!"

"You are a burnt child, so every stove makes you nervous," Uncle Luis protests. "I am a man who has played with fire all his life."

"Playing is one thing," my father observes. "Crawling into the hot oven and pulling the door shut is another." As he rolls a cigarette, he adds, "Forgive me. I am not one to give advice. I have made more mistakes than anybody."

He rises slowly, standing beside me, looking around the one room of our house. Many years ago my mother ran away with the lettuce picker from Imperial Valley. Since then there has been only my papa and Uncle Luis and me. But we have always had more fun together than anybody.

"Pedro," my father says sadly, "there are times when a man feels very helpless."

My Uncle Luis, who has been on the bed, puts both feet on the floor. He is searching for his shoes. Until we remind him, he does not remember that he has left them in Manuel Velez's barbershop this morning.

"I am still a free man," he grumbles. "I do exactly what I choose to do."

"A fish which bites a nice live bait is also a free fish," my father says, "but not for long."

"A stupid example," Uncle Luis growls. "Señora Murphy is not a frisky anchovy. She is more in the nature of a big aquarium. The water is a nice temperature, and the food is good. From such a place one can watch the world go by. Also, there are other considerations which I can not discuss."

He takes his hat from the nail on the door, and pats my father's shoulder. "A widow is a good investment, José. You will see."

"*Caramba!*" my father cries. "She is selling you a restaurant in which you will be only the dishwasher. Luis, this woman is trouble on the hoof!"

"Think of it!" Uncle Luis replies. "Tonight she is broiling me a fine lobster with plenty of hot butter. A nice avocado salad — a big artichoke — a bottle of cool *vino* —" He stands rubbing his stomach, and my mouth is watering as if I am beside him at the table.

"Get out!" my father shouts. "You speak like a turkey the day before Thanksgiving."

"Remember your shoes at Manuel Velez's," I remind him.

"This boy is the love of my heart, José," he says. "With a rich uncle like myself behind him, he could become governor of California some day."

When he is gone, my father stands shaking his head. "Pedro," he says, " a man like our Luis does not change so quickly. It is unnatural. For two weeks he has not even been on the pier to use the grappling hook for small salvage. He has picked up no spare automobile parts. He has not brought home a single chicken which was lost. In Luis such virtue is a dangerous disease. This woman is using a tool on him which we do not understand."

"He likes to eat," I say.

"He has liked to eat before," he replies.

"She is a widow."

"There have been other widows."

"Maybe it's love."

"Of course — love," my father says thoughtfully. "But love of what? Señora Murphy is a very strong woman. A strict woman. Her hair is always combed too perfect, and she is full of arguments. That is why Tim Murphy is under the ground. It is well known that she made him so mad one day that he swung the iron ball on his wrecking crane in a big circle with such force that his machine was upset and he was killed. Such a woman is not for Luis."

I think my father is right. I know this troublesome Señora Murphy very well, and I do not doubt that she is one to make people mad. She is a heavy-stacked woman with narrow black eyes who walks as if she is carrying a water crock on her head.

"Why does she make people mad?" I ask.

"She is a reformer," my father says. "She is a person who forgives nothing and who tries to change everything. She is the one who complains of flies in the bakery. She is the one who made Manuel Velez stop sweeping his barbershop hair on the sidewalk. She is the one who went to Father Lomita about changing the holy water in the Church font more often."

"I know," I say. "She gave me a toothbrush and tried to make me scrub. I sold it to Paco Velez for a nickel to use with his shoe polish."

"That's what I mean," my father nods. "She is after everybody like a grave digger with a new shovel."

My father often explains things to me if he thinks I do not understand. He says it is important for stupid people to be polite and not step on toes.

"I think she is trying to reform our Luis," he goes on. "She has found a weak spot, and is mixing business with pleasure. She is a woman who would drain the whole ocean if she thought there was one small pearl on the bottom."

While we are talking, a knock rattles the door. The next minute pretty Carmelita Smith is standing before us, shaking my Uncle Luis' guitar by the neck. She is part gypsy, and when she is mad she is hotter than a parrot full of peppercorns.

"Where's Luis?" she demands.

My father shrugs. "He just stepped out."

"The bum!" she cries. "I'll wrap this box around his neck!" She explains if my Uncle Luis had any brains he would have them out on the sidewalk playing with them.

"Has he done something wrong?" my father inquires.

"You tell me!" she says. "For two weeks he hasn't been near my house."

"I'll take the guitar," my father says mildly. "A guitar should be played often to keep the tone sweet."

"It's that Florencia Murphy!" she explodes. "My enchiladas and tortillas are not good enough for Luis anymore. That woman is spending her dead husband's insurance money like water to butter him up. This afternoon in the market it was lobsters and artichokes and special little jars of heaven knows what! He is like a rooster picking up corn behind her!"

"Sit down, Carmelita," my father says. "Pedro, place the chair for Carmelita."

When I have put the orange crate under her with politeness, she takes my face in her hands and rubs her nose to mine because I am a sweet little banana.

"Perhaps if you keep the guitar," my father suggests, "Luis will stop by after supper to play a little."

All of a sudden she is blazing again. "The lousy bum!" she says. "For years we have fought it to a draw with each other. Now he throws himself away on an itchy broad who has hardly raised a finger except to cross herself. I can not under-stand it! It is an unspeakable insult to me!"

"Luis must have a reason," my father answers. "I am as troubled about it as you are. As I told Pedro before you came in, she must be using a tool on him which we do not understand."

"There is no tool in the box which some woman has not used on Luis," she says. "He is not a man to marry, and I have respected his point of view. So we dance and fight and have fun slitting each other's throats."

"I know," my father says.

"How can a man be so smart with one woman, and so stupid with another? I respected his independence. Now he turns into a monkey on a string for her! I hate him!" She whirls to leave.

"Here," my father says gently. "Take this home again with you." He lays the guitar in her hands. "As long as you have something which belongs to another, it is like a little thread which remains unbroken."

"I don't want it!" she cries. "It's all over between us!"

But finally she is persuaded. "That's better," my father says. "If things go badly, you can always sell it and buy a new dress."

She stands hugging the guitar.

"I'll buy something, allright," she promises, "but I'll need a police permit to carry it!"

"A lovely girl," my father observes, when Carmelita is gone. "She and Luis are two of a kind. Such a friendship is a beautiful thing."

"I know," I say.

Because Carmelita was too upset to speak to me, it does not mean that we are not good friends, too. At the Caliente Café, where she is cashier, she gives me many good things to eat. And whenever I have something which must be hidden from my father and Uncle Luis she takes care of it for me. Often when my Uncle Luis plays his guitar to her I sit with them on her porch and it is one of the nicest things which happens.

"If Uncle Luis gets married to Señora Murphy, that's the end of Carmelita, isn't it?" I ask.

"I'm afraid so," my father sighs. "It is also the end of a very happy time in this house."

"Will Señora Murphy come to live with us?"

"A woman who lives in an apartment over a poultry store will move at the first chance," he answers. "This is only a one room house on the alley in back of an empty lot, but it is better than being on top of a chicken coop."

"But what will happen to you and me, Papa?"

"A good question," my father groans. "We will be two grains of wheat between the millstones."

I have once heard Father Lomita speak in Church concerning these millstones. They grind slowly and very fine. But my Uncle Luis has explained that nine hundred million Chinamen know that it takes only one grain of wheat to keep the millstones apart.

While I repeat this to my father we have our supper of two mackerel I have caught on the Santa Monica pier today and a loaf of bread which was given to us by the bus driver who found it under a seat at the end of his run.

"Perhaps we do not live right," my father says thoughtfully. "Now that you mention Father Lomita, I think I will go to him tomorrow and offer to cut the Church grass. If Señora Murphy has spoken to him about Luis, perhaps he will speak of it to me."

"I'll bet he won't," I say. "The Padre keeps his lip buttoned on what people tell him."

"Just the same," my father continues, "if a marriage is hanging over our heads, we should find out just how bad things are. Tonight I would like to be a bug on the wall of Señora Murphy's apartment."

"She would squash you dead," I answer. "You always say little pitchers have big ears. If I go out and cruise around, I might hear something."

My father studies me for a minute. "I see no harm in that," he says, "but one should not be a spy."

"No, sir."

"And if you find yourself on the stairs behind the poultry store, be very careful. The stairs are rotten and make a bad noise."

"Yes, sir."

"And don't wake the chickens."

"For Pete's sake!" I protest. "You'd think I never—"

"Allright," he nods. "Just be a good boy. Keep out of trouble."

I know the back of Señor Santee's poultry store like my tongue knows my teeth. Señor Santee lives upstairs in the front, and Señora Murphy lives in the back. Chicken crates are stacked by the stairs which go up to her back landing with the garbage can and the umbrella pole where she hangs her wash. Inside the windows are her little kitchen and the room of her apartment. The big room window is open for air.

I keep my bare feet close to the building edge of the stairs. In no time I am sitting on the garbage can, peeping in through a corner of the window curtain.

My Uncle Luis and Señora Murphy are sitting at the table. A great platter of red lobster carcasses is between them. On the table is an empty wine bottle and my Uncle Luis is leaning back, a toothpick in one hand and a fat cigar in the other.

"Florencia," he says, "tonight you have surpassed yourself. This dinner, she was from heaven."

Since this dinner was maybe from Señor Tim Murphy's insurance money, I consider my Uncle Luis has said the truth. Señora Murphy has her hair piled up like black tar. Her rings flash with fire as she holds out the candle to light my Uncle Luis' cigar.

"For you, Luis," she says, "nothing is too good." In a sticky voice, she declares, "It is a pleasant thing to have a little money when it brings happiness to lonely people."

She explains to my Uncle Luis how it is an unfair world in which men pass away before women. Because of this, the women own most of the property in the country. They have more votes than men at election time. They do all the important buying which keeps business good.

"Every widow has the obligation to marry again," she says. "It is a delightful way to restore equality to men and to divide the wealth." She is leaning across to my Uncle Luis as if he is her answer to everything. "There are so few men of sensibility," she sighs. "So few who understand these matters."

My Uncle Luis, who has never owned anything but his guitar and a small grappling hook to fish junk from under the pier, studies the ash on his cigar.

"Money does not interest me," he says modestly. "There is only myself, my brother, and my small nephew. We live simply and devote our leisure time to music and the humanities."

"Of course," she says. "You are a man of culture."

"But I am not a happy man," he continues. "It is my small nephew, Pedro, who distresses me. He is the apple of my eye. But he is at that time of life when a woman's influence is important. He should have security. You have read in the papers about the juvenile delinquents—gang fights— stealings—killings. Without a woman in the family to guide him, I fear for our little Pedro." He bows his head as if I am lying dead in a small casket on the table before him.

Caramba! He's nuts! I think. *He has lost his head with all his marbles in it!*

Señora Murphy slides from her chair. "That is one worry I can lift from your shoulders!" she cries with eagerness. She has the same look on her face as when she tried to poke the toothbrush down my throat. "Luis," she declares, "you are not only a handsome man with brains, but you have heart—a great heart!"

"Florencia," he sighs, "for the first time in my life, I am tempted to be respectable." He takes her hand.

Suddenly, he lets go, and is holding his mouth as if he is going to throw up. He reaches for his pocket as if he is going to blow his nose.

"Luis—you were going to say something?" she encourages.

"It was nothing," he mumbles. He is standing still, staring down at a small object which he has drawn from his pants pocket.

"What is it, Luis?" Señora Murphy begs. "Is it a ring?"

"My guitar pick," he says slowly. He is holding it between his thumb and forefinger like a bug which has been biting him. "This pick has been worn thin with making sweet music," he adds.

"Of course!" Señora Murphy says with coolness. "Why did I not think of music before?" She disappears out of the light, and there is the start of a smaltzy record on her phonograph. "Come here, Luis," I hear her say. "Come sit by me on the sofa."

My Uncle Luis kicks at the table leg and scratches his head. Finally, he shrugs and moves out of the light too. Now I can see nothing beyond the candles. The screwy music is too loud to hear anything.

Caramba! I think. *If he stretches his neck for more of that stuff he is a dead turkey.*.

I run all the way home. When I am through the door, my father sits on the table. Jesús Rinaldo, the gambler, is stretched on the bed, and Manuel Velez is on the apple box. Two-finger Jones, who takes bets on the horses, sits with his arms spread to make points. He is croaking in his big voice like a bull toad.

"Jesús is telling you right, José," he says. "When this Murphy number visited her sister in Arcadia last month, they went the the Santa Anita track every day. She dropped a bundle on the nags. Maybe all she had. For two weeks she hasn't sneaked even a two-buck bet with me. I tell you, she's broke."

"We thought Luis should know," Manuel says. "It is too bad he has invested so much time with her."

"Papa!" I cry, before anybody else can talk. "Señora Murphy is laying it on to Uncle Luis with a shovel. They are telling big lies to each other. She already has him on the sofa." I relate what has happened as fast as I can.

"What'd I say," Jesús Rinaldo observes. "Maybe next it's the bed. She is a desperate woman, baiting the trap with her last piece of cheese."

"A hypocrite," Manuel adds. "A brain washer with a secret sin, who wants to make everything clean all the time."

"If she had dropped her dough with me, I wouldn't criticize her," Two-finger Jones croaks. "But this dame should be rendered inactive. I vote we knock her joint over and pull Luis out of bed."

My father begs for quiet. "Luis is a proud man," he says. "If we rush to him now and say what we know, he will feel a great fool. Such a mistake is hard to live down."

"If he asks her to marry him and then backs out, such a woman will sue him for breach of promise," Jesús Rinaldo warns. "He will have to face a judge. Which kind of disgrace is worst?"

"We could set fire to Santee's poultry store," Manuel offers hopefully.

"Señor Santee is a violent man," my father protests. "The innocent should not be made to suffer."

"Let us go to Nick Aliso's bar where we can think better," Jesús Rinaldo suggests. "After a few drinks, maybe everything will not be so impossible."

My father instructs me to go to bed. The others bat me around a little, like good friends, before they file out the door.

"Say your prayers and remember our Uncle Luis," my father calls back.

I wait until they are gone. Then I tear out for Carmelita Smith's house. It would be a sin to go to bed when maybe I can help my Uncle Luis.

When I bust in upon her, Carmelita is standing in her bra and panties ironing a red petticoat. There is a dish of icecream on the ironing board.

"Get yourself a saucer," she waves to me. "There is more in the icebox."

"Do you know why Señora Murphy is trying to hook Uncle Luis?" I demand.

The iron stops. She slams it on end. "Darling," she says, "what woman wouldn't?" Then she becomes angry. "I'll tell you why! She wants to latch on to three men to work for her! She has a little money and she is looking for an investment. She wants somebody to boss around, now Tim Murphy is at peace. It is as simple as that!"

"She hasn't any money anymore!" I cry.

I report all that Two-finger Jones has said, and everything I have seen looking into the back window of Señora Murphy's apartment.

"He was almost ready to ask her to get married," I say, "when he chickened out. He thinks he ought to have security and be respectable on account of me."

"You are a big-eared little angel!" she exclaims. She sweeps me into her arms. "Tell me again how he looked at the guitar pick! Was he very, very miserable?"

I repeat what I have seen. "It was like he had caught a pinchbug in his pants," I explain.

"He was thinking of me!" she cries. "He was remembering his guitar and all our good times together."

She flings the petticoat over her head and grabs her dress from the closet.

"His guitar is in the bedroom on the bed," she says. "Run get it! Poor sweet Luis! The stupid jerk! Respectable, my eye!"

When I bring her Uncle Luis' guitar, I am struck with terror. She is sticking a little dagger into the top of her stocking. She is blazing out a stream of words in gypsy talk.

"Take Luis' guitar to your father at Nick's saloon," she instructs. "Tell them to play it when Murphy's ghost flies over."

I have never seen Carmelita so mad. She snatches me into her arms and squeezes me tight.

"You will always be my little *caballero*," she says, "even if I go to prison. Now scram to your papa!"

I run all the way to Nick Aliso's saloon and elbow through the pool players to the crowd at the bar who are shouting and laughing around my father.

"Carmelita is going to kill Señora Murphy!" I cry. I press the guitar into his hands. "She says to play this when Murphy's ghost flies over."

There is a great silence as I repeat what has happened at Carmelita's. Jesús Rinaldo slides out his empty glass, and Nick Aliso pours without being asked.

When nobody will speak first, Tadpole Garmo, who is a shoemaker and musician, takes the guitar from my father and runs a few soft chords to *Adios, Mariquita Linda*. "Maybe Luis' ghost will fly over, too," he says presently.

With Tadpole's words, my father cries that we must all do something. "What if we were in Luis' shoes?" he asks.

Now the whole saloon is shouting. Everybody grabs what is loose, and there is a great push. Nick Aliso is bawling to leave the pool sticks behind before everybody kills somebody.

It is like a fire, with people shouting and running in the night. All of Pico Street is sticking its head out, with nightshirts and pajamas everyplace. Jesús Rinaldo is shouting at the top of his lungs that there is a murder at Santee's poultry store, upstairs in the apartment.

My father grips my arm when we get there. "Around to the back stairs—fast!" he instructs.

I think we are already too late. Glass is crashing from Señora Murphy's window as a bottle flies out. Then everything is coming through. Dishes. Cushions. Señora Murphy's portable phonograph. There are women's screams. Suddenly, the window goes dark and the floor lamp comes through. A howling has set off the chickens. Señor Santee is roaring from his window like a crazy landlord.

"There is no sound from Luis," my father cries. "He is lying already with a knife in his ribs!"

"I have not heard such a noise since my marriage," Nick Aliso shouts happily, as we push past him. He has put the tasseled lampshade on his head. Everybody has forgotten my Uncle Luis. They are all shouting for Carmelita to throw Señora Murphy out on her ear.

My father and I jump together for the back stairs to reach the landing. There is a screech of nails as the steps pull apart from the wall. The next minute we are crashing into the chicken crates with the garbage can and clothes pole upon us.

"Are you hurt?" my father cries in the darkness.

"I'm allright."

"I, too," he says. "Listen—hear that siren? We must stack up these crates. Try to reach the door. We must get our Luis out before the police come!"

"Hey—José—Pedro!" It is a weak voice from under the chicken crates. "It's me—Luis! Pull me out!"

When we have pulled him loose, he says he has dived from the landing and knocked himself cold as he hit the crates. "I thought the chickens would be softer," he explains.

"Thank God!" my father says. "We thought Carmelita had put a knife in you!"

"What knife?" Uncle Luis asks with fright. "When she broke in the front door, I went out the back."

"She had a knife," I tell him. "Her little gypsy dagger. She was after Señora Murphy."

"*Caramba!*" Uncle Luis shouts. "I know that little stickeroo." He is already helping us throw up crates like a crazy man. "We must stop her!" he cries. "I thought she was after me."

Before my father can hold him, he has climbed on the crates. He scrambles up and throws himself into the door.

"After him!" my father commands. "If something bad has happened, we must all stand together with Carmelita."

We have both heard the police siren coming near. Many people are already crowding upon us as we leap up the crates.

Inside, in the darkness, my father pushes me behind him. He goes first. We see my Uncle Luis putting a match to a candle. A big roar goes up from the outside when everybody sees the light.

It is a terrible sight that is before us.

Carmelita is sitting on top of Señora Murphy on the floor and is laughing until she can not stop. She is waving her arm over her head. In her hand is a big bunch of something like black tar. It is Señora Murphy's hair.

"It's a wig!" she cries. "Look, Luis! It's a wig! She's baldheaded!"

The Señora is struggling to hide her bald head. She begs Carmelita not to hurt the precious wig. To please not tell anybody. She will do anything. Only please don't disgrace her before the whole neighborhood.

"The police!" my father cries. "They will be up here any minute!"

In quick words he whispers to Uncle Luis what Jesús Rinaldo has said about the Señora. "She is a fake. A sneaky gambler besides," he says. "Two-finger Jones will swear to it."

It is with great tenderness that Uncle Luis pulls Carmelita off from the top of the Señora.

"Everybody must do exactly as I say," he commands.

My Uncle Luis is all at once a great general in charge of everything.

When the two policemen pound on the door and barge in upon us, we are all sitting on the sofa, in candle light. We are breaking up little lobster legs and laughing as we lick our fingers.

"What the hell is going on here?" the biggest cop demands.

"A small informal party," my Uncle Luis replies.

Señora Murphy stands up very snooty, touching her black hair with her ringed fingers. "Has there been a complaint about the noise, Officer?"

"Complaint!" the cop yells. "Half of Pico Street is outside! It's a crazy mob. Broken furniture all over the place. They say somebody's been stabbed."

"There's no broken furniture here," Uncle Luis says. "Look for yourself."

It is true. Everything is all straight in the room. We have pitched the broken stuff out the window.

"The Señora is not a rich woman," my father explains mildly. "If this room is a little bare, you should not embarrass her."

"You're all *loco!*" the policeman explodes. "We ought to take you all in!"

"But why?" Uncle Luis shrugs. "A few friends are celebrating because they think maybe there is going to be an engagement." He pats Carmelita's hand which is in his. "It is always a possibility," he adds.

"At such a time, you understand how it is," my father says. He moves to stand politely beside the door. "A little privacy is hard to find these days."

"Sure," the cop says uncertainly. "Sure." He nudges his partner. "Let's leave well enough alone."

When they are gone, Carmelita and Señora Murphy glare at each other again.

My father hurries to lean from the window.

"Tadpole!" he calls down. "Do you still have Luis' guitar?" When a shout comes up from Tadpole Garmo, he asks for a little music.

"Everything is all settled!" he informs everybody.

From below the broken windows there is the sound of my Uncle Luis' guitar. Soon the whole street is singing. When the police siren howls away, we know it is the right time for us to go.

At the door, my Uncle Luis bends over Señora Murphy's hand. "It was a delightful dinner," he says.

My father bows. Only Carmelita makes a move as if she will snatch Señora Murphy baldheaded again.

"From now on, keep your hands off my Luis," she says.

"And you keep your mouth shut about my hair and my finances," the Señora retorts.

When I have said goodnight, too, we all go down the hallway. We tiptoe past Señor Santee who is wringing his hands like a suffering landlord who is too full to speak.

"A night to remember," my father whispers to me.

"Ouch!" my Uncle Luis howls. He leaps from the stairs halfway down to the street.

Behind him Carmelita breaks into laughter. She lifts her red petticoat and returns the little dagger to its place.

"You see, Pedro, how it goes in these matters," my father says softly. "A man who loves freedom should never look for security."

THE PINK ANGEL

Pepe Monterey, luckiest young man on all of Pico Street, sat in the gloom of the Casa Grande Café, holding his aching head. Beside him stood Father Lomita, patient but unsmiling.

"This is the last day of the year," Father Lomita reminded him sternly, looking down at the wine-stained wood of the table which supported the elbows of his prodigal sheep. "You have not yet provided the headstone for your Uncle Tito's grave."

"The pink angel!" cried the consciense-stricken Pepe, leaping up. "I will get it this very minute, father!"

The priest frowned. "I have reminded you repeatedly. The months have passed. There are only a few hours left, Pepe."

"I will not slip this time, sure . . . I promise," the penitent one replied.

"For some things you have not much of a memory," the priest said, relenting a little. "When you go to Señor La Paz for the stone, think only of your Uncle Tito, and not of the money it costs. You will not forget, Pepe?"

"I will not forget," Pepe replied humbly.

"It is for the good of your own soul," the priest said, "that you must carry out your Uncle Tito's request."

"Yes, father," Pepe answered.

"I am going to the cemetery tomorrow morning early," Father Lomita said. "I will expect to see that you have fulfilled your obligation." He laid a protecting hand briefly on Pepe's black, curly head. Then he walked placidly through the room, nodding to Nick Aliso behind the bar and lifting a gentle finger to such others of his flock as he saw there.

But when the priest's broad back had passed into the warm sunlight of Pico Street, Pepe relaxed into the chair from which he had recently leaped, and a sleepy smile overspread his brown features. He yawned with luxurious indifference. He polished his fingernails on the breast of his bright shirt. He turned over his empty glass and pushed it from him. The others in the room said nothing.

Pepe stretched his legs before him and stared at the alarm clock on the bar shelf. Four o'clock. He had not much time, but after such a public reminder by Father Lomita, a decent interval of indifference was required for the restoration of his dignity in the eyes of his friends.

This was understood and expected. Luis Gonzalez, who stood by the pinball machine, observed that it was a fine day for feeling good. Nick Aliso took a slug from the cash register and fed it into the juke box. When a South American rhythm filled the room, all present sank into respectful attitudes of absorption.

Presently, with a show of infinite boredom, Pepe rose from the table. "See you tomorrow," he yawned, and sauntered in the general direction of the door. The others followed him approvingly with their eyes.

But once outside, Pepe broke into a run. The music pounded behind him, heightening the tempo of his distress. He sped through the dust to the bumperless and fenderless vehicle that waited in a vacant weed-grown lot. It was not a hot-rod, this car of Pepe's. It was a deceased hot-rod, from which time and accident had drained both heat and vitality. It was a mere ghost of transportation — a collection of corroded plumbing from which the upholstery stuffing protruded like heads of cauliflowers. Pepe flung himself into the ancient wreck, and after a few preliminary disappointments, rattled off in the direction of Señor La Paz's marble and granite works.

Now, Pepe's uncle, Tito Monterey, who was the remote cause of Pepe's present haste, had been a man of gigantic good humor. During a time of widespread economic depression, he had lost his left leg to the richest railroad in all of Southern California. It had been the joke of his life. Thereafter, for many years, he had sat in the shade of the pepper tree in his yard, like a great oak-purple wine cask, slapping his cork leg and recounting his good fortune. In his mind it had been a magnificent illustration of justice that the gringos, who had stolen California, had been forced to settle with him for a sum worthy of a Spanish don.

As a child, Pepe had delighted his uncle greatly. For example, when Uncle Tito changed his socks each week, Pepe was allowed to hammer in the tacks that held up the fresh sock on the "golden leg." As he grew older, it was Pepe who maneuvered strangers to sit at his uncle's left side. In telling some ribald story, the old man would roar with laughter, slapping his listener's knee. When, in happy excitement, the listeners slapped back, they came near breaking their hands on cork and steel.

All of life had been a great jest to Uncle Tito, and in this atmosphere of worldly merriment Pepe had flourished to the age of twenty-three like a tough tomato plant in the middle of a well-traveled garden walk. While more carefully planted boys grew timid and serious, Pepe had grown hardy and full of laughter. His uncle loved him. But one night, a few months past, Uncle Tito had made his last joke. He had called for Father Lomita and made his peace. He had commanded the priest to keep a faithful eye on Pepe. And he had instructed Pepe to place the cork leg in a box that had been made ready, and mail it back to the railroad.

Thus it was that Pepe had inherited a small sum of money and become known as the luckiest young man on all Pico Street. And thus it was that Father Lomita kept a particularly watchful eye over him. Furthermore, it was not without deep concern that the priest had sought him out at the Casa Grande Café and sternly reminded him of his somber responsibility in the matter of the headstone.

For Uncle Tito had left a letter with Father Lomita, which the latter had duly delivered to Pepe. It contained the old man's dying wish. The letter recalled to his nephew's mind the beautiful, pink-marble angel that stood like a laughing child among the gray shafts and stones of Señor La Paz's monument yard. Uncle Tito had desired that before the year of his death was passed Pepe should secure this pink angel and place it upon his grave. It was his last and only request. If Pepe did not do this, the letter ended, his Uncle Tito would personally take care of him from the next world. In the meantime, Pepe would answer in the matter to Father Lomita.

It was a clear letter. It had been dictated to the priest and signed by Uncle Tito. It had taken full account of Pepe's gay and irresponsible nature. But, as had been expected, Pepe had put the thing off. Father Lomita had chided him repeatedly. Pepe had found excuses: It was a sad business; it cost a great deal of money; perhaps Uncle Tito had been joking; allright, then, he would do it the next time he passed Señor La Paz's shop. But he had not done it. Time, like the priest's patience, had run out. And now, with only a few hours remaining in the year, Pepe bent over the rattling steering wheel of his decrepit jalopy, forced, at last into doing the good thing.

However, when he saw slender María Flores in her fresh white blouse and wide black skirt emerge from the bakery shop, he swung the wheel and careened about in a full stream of traffic amid a screech of brakes, sliding tires and shouted imprecations from all sides.

"Taxi, señorita?" he cried, shuddering to a stop beside her.

María tossed her head. Even the red carnation in her hair seemed to stiffen. She held the white cake box delicately by its string. But she stopped. "Please do not annoy me," she said haughtily. "I am in a hurry."

"But María," Pepe protested. "My darling, I have been looking for you everywhere."

"Do not call me 'darling' . . . ever again!" The heels of her small slippers rattled like castanets on the sidewalk. "You — you never remember anything!"

But Pepe had remembered — the instant he had seen her. "If you mean about the New Year's dance tonight," he said lamely, "I thought we settled it."

"You never opened your big mouth!" María cried. "I haven't even seen you since the Christmas party!"

"I thought I did," he said vaguely. "Why else would I have ordered a big corsage of gardenias for you?" He looked devoutly to heaven. "It is my Uncle Tito's gravestone that has confused me — there have been many things to look after."

"Oh, I'm sorry," María said instantly. "If it was on account of Uncle Tito that you forgot — "

"I am on my way now to Señor La Paz's monument yard," he said, sighing deeply, "to get the stone and take it to Uncle Tito's resting place."

But there was still a doubt in María's eyes. "I heard you have been celebrating on Soto Street in Los Angeles. They say you bought toys for all the kids and made everybody drunk for three days."

"I have no recollection of such a thing," Pepe answered righteously. "People talk about me because I have a little money. It is the same everywhere. Just read the papers."

"Soon," María said firmly, "you will have as little money as you have memory."

"What's in the cake box?" Pepe said abruptly.

"Nothing," María replied, looking a little sheepish.

"For tonight — for us?" Pepe grinned.

"Well," María admitted, "it is possible."

"Soon as I take care of Uncle Tito and go to the barber shop, I'll be by," Pepe promised. "Nine o'clock?"

"Nine o'clock," María murmured.

"I love you," Pepe smiled, his black eyes sparkling.

"Please . . . don't forget . . . tonight," María begged.

Had he looked again as he whirled the car about in the street, Pepe might has seen María's lovely lips despairingly form the words, "You sweet liar! You big bum!" But his mind was already directed to carrying out his promise.

His first stop was at the Hoja Verde Flower Shop to shout the belated order for the gardenia corsage to Goyo Moreno. From there it was only half a block to Señor La Paz's monument yard.

The old stone cutter, his mallet across his lap, was sleeping in the doorway at the rear of his small shop. Pepe hurried to him and tapped his shoulder. "Señor—Señor La Paz!"

The old man awakened slowly, smiling half in dream and half in recognition of Pepe, who, by this time was staring fixedly and unbelievingly, not at the old man, but at a little square of bare earth edged with chickweed among the jumble of slabs and shafts.

"Señor La Paz!" he shouted excitedly, shaking the old man's shoulder. "It's gone! The pink angel is gone!"

Señor La Paz nodded brightly. "It is good to see you, Pepe. How is your Uncle Tito?" Because he did not hear well, he had missed the sense of Pepe's outcry. And since events in the near present no longer recorded well in his mind, therefore Uncle Tito remained alive in his memory.

Pepe explained slowly and distinctly all that concerned Uncle Tito and the headstone, ending desperately, "Señor, where has it gone? Who bought it? What did you do with it?"

"For twenty years it sat there in my yard and no one wanted it," Señor La Paz mused. "You used to play around it, Pepe, when you were little. It was no bigger than yourself."

"I know, señor!" Pepe cried. "But for the love of heaven, where is it now?"

"Every year I made the price lower," the old man continued, "but nobody wanted it. Nobody could pay for Italian marble. It was a beautiful mistake."

"Yes, I know!" Pepe answered. "But where is it?"

Señor La Paz regarded him sadly. "I am an old man. If I had kept it, my son would have used it on me someday. And it was too good for me." He shook his head disapprovingly. "Much too good!"

Pepe sank on the steps beside him. "Señor, I must have that pink angel!" he cried into his ear. "No matter where it is or who has got it. I must have it!"

"To the young, everything is a crisis," the old man smiled. "Do you know a gringo who is called T. S. Cutler?"

"I have never heard the name," Pepe replied.

"I sold it to him," the old man said, "not a week ago. He is going to make a great thing of it in his garden."

"Where does he live?" Pepe cried.

"I was very fond of your Uncle Tito," Señor La Paz said dreamily. "He was not a predictable man. He made many jokes on the gringos." The old man shook his head thoughtfully. "Perhaps now a gringo will make a joke on Uncle Tito."

"Yes, yes!" Pepe replied frantically. "Only tell me where to find this T. S. Cutler."

Señor La Paz rose stiffly and went to the corner of his shop where he kept his dusty account book. "Yes, here it is," he said presently. "T. S. Cutler . . . in Beverly Hills."

Pepe snatched up a scrap of paper and scribbled down the address. "How much did he pay you for it?" he demanded. "It will cost me at least that much to get it away from him."

"It is a question," Señor La Paz said doubtfully. "He was going to bore a hole through it for a water spout from the mouth. A beautiful thought. Perhaps it broke in pieces."

"But how much did he pay you?" Pepe cried.

Señor La Paz ran his finger across the page, an amused smile on his gentle face. "Two hundred and fifty dollars," he said.

"Oh, no!" Pepe cried helplessly. "I have only two hundred dollars left to my name!"

"A pity," Señor La Paz nodded. "But perhaps the gringo has broke it in pieces anyway."

"Do not say that, señor," Pepe moaned. "It is a terrible thought."

"At the same time, it would be a fine joke on your Uncle Tito," Señor La Paz remarked dryly. "It was a vanity—this pink angel!"

Pepe rushed from the monument shop and threw himself into his battered car. Beverly Hills lay several miles away, and his destination was a strange street for which he would have to search. Rounding a corner, turning east from Sepulveda Boulevard, a rear tire blew out, and he set to work replacing it with another ragged carcass which he unearthed from a jumble of junk in the rear of the car. Having no jack, he backed to the side of the road, slipped a wooden block under the axle and, using a short spade he carried for that purpose, dug a trench under the wheel. With a short crowbar and a spring leaf, he removed the tire and patched the long slit in the tube.

It was hard work and took time. When he had finished, he found himself famished. Darkness had fallen. Devouring a hamburger at a lunch stand, he sped on, grimly apprehensive of the unknown Mr. Cutler. Besides, he was filled with misery that the canvas belt around his waist contained only two hundred dollars. It was all that remained of Uncle Tito's legacy, and it fell far short of his needs. Perhaps the gringo would accept the car for fifty dollars. Yet how would he bring back the pink angel without the car? Despair gripped him, but he rattled on.

Filling the radiator and inquiring directions at a gasoline station, he chanced to see a one-legged man leaning on a white crutch under a palm tree. His heart stopped, momentarily, as he thought of Uncle Tito. By the time he had driven out of the station, the man had disappeared. A cold sweat bathed his brow. The broad avenue, overhung with trees, into which he now turned, might have been a black tunnel of purgatory, illumined at intervals by the hot lights of Christmas trees.

He missed the residence of T. S. Cutler once, thinking the solid, vine-covered structure was a branch of the public library. Finally, when he rattled into the drive and tiptoed between the stone lions and along the colored mosaic tile of the entrance, he felt indeed as if he were seeking the devil himself.

A butler opened the door. Pepe saw his cold eyes flash over him, taking in his clothes, his dirty hands and rumpled hair, and coming to a bad conclusion.

"Señor . . . you are Señor Cutler?" Pepe cried. "I must see Señor Cutler!"

"Mr. Cutler is occupied," the butler said curtly. "Please go away." He moved to close the door.

At which Pepe set up such a howl in explanation of the pink angel, the gravestone, Uncle Tito and his own misery that the reserve of the man before him was completely shattered. "The grave of my Uncle Tito has been robbed!" he cried. "A terrible mistake has been made! If you do not let me see Señor Cutler, Uncle Tito will send an earthquake and shake this house down!"

"I am Mr. Cutler," an amused voice said. The butler stood aside, and a tall, gray-haired man with tiny, turned-up mustaches and twinkling blue eyes surveyed Pepe from head to foot.

"Señor," Pepe began, "you bought a pink angel on Pico Street. It is my Uncle Tito's tombstone. It is for one who is dead. If the kind señor had but known, he would not have done this terrible thing."

Mr. Cutler grew very grave, and his tiny mustaches twitched vigorously. "I did, indeed, buy a piece of quaint statuary on Pico Street," he said. "Step inside and we will discuss it, if you like."

"But, sir!" coughed the butler.

"Turn on the lights in the garden," Mr. Cutler said. "This gentleman and I may want to go there presently . . . Your name, sir?"

"Pepe Monterey," Pepe gulped. "But there is little time, señor—if you please, señor—I want to buy it back from you—the statuary. It is a matter of life and death, señor. Mostly death," he ended plaintively.

"Come; you will tell me your story," Mr. Cutler said, guiding him politely into the drawing room. He instructed the butler, who still stood irresolutely, to bring them sherry wine. "My family has gone out tonight," he said. "You will begin at the beginning, Mr. Monterey, and give me all the details." Waving the frantic Pepe to the huge sofa, he drew up a great chair facing the coffee table between them. Settling himself comfortably, he offered Pepe a cigar.

"No, señor, tonight it would make me sick," Pepe said, sitting on the sofa's edge. "You see, señor, it is like this—"

The butler appeared with decanter and glasses on a tray. Mr. Cutler held up a finger. "First, a glass of wine," he said. "Then we will get into the story."

"But please, señor!" Pepe begged. "I am in a hurry! María is waiting! Uncle Tito is pounding his leg in heaven! Father Lomita maybe is saying words on me!"

"So there is a girl, too, as well as an uncle. And a priest!" Mr. Cutler sank back in the chair, as if all the thousand and one tales of the Arabian Nights lay before him. "You may begin, Señor Monterey." he said, closing his eyes.

"In the name of heaven, señor!" Pepe cried, wringing his hands. "Do not fall asleep!" And with that he began pouring forth the story, beginning with Uncle Tito and the railroad, forgetting important points, going back, starting afresh, adding material as needed to persuade, lamenting his own misery as that of a grasshopper overtaken by winter, and pounding the pillow beside him as if it were Uncle Tito's august member of cork and steel. "If I lie, Señor Cutler," he

ended bravely, "you may pick me bald-headed, one hair at
a time!"

Mr. Cutler opened his eyes and regarded Pepe intently.
"Remarkable!" he said. "Astonishing!"

Pepe bethought himself then of Uncle Tito's letter, and
with trembling fingers drew the creased and soiled document
from his billfold, spreading it for Mr. Cutler to read. It bore
the witnessing signature of Father Lomita, and it was written on the stationery of the church. "If you knew my Uncle
Tito like I do," Pepe said, "the next world is the last place
on earth you would dare to go. It will not be safe even for you
to die, señor!"

"Come," Mr. Cutler said, rising. His tiny gray mustaches
were erect and twitching. "Let's have a look in the garden."
He led the way outside and along the formal, box-hedged
path to a heap of stones where a shallow pool was being
constructed.

"There it is!" Pepe cried, rushing to where the pink angel
lay on a mound of sand. "Thank heaven, señor, you have not
put the hole through it!" In a burst of excitement he lifted it
in his arms. "You will sell it back to me, señor?"

He saw Mr. Cutler smile and wave aside the butler, who
had suddenly appeared from nowhere. "It was rather foolishly
expensive," Mr. Cutler said wryly. "Two hundred and fifty
dollars."

"With your permission," Pepe said, trembling. He set the
angel on a bench, pulled up his shirt and untied the canvas
belt from around his waist. He took out four sadly creased
fifty-dollar bills. "This is all I have left in the world, señor,"
he said. "This and my automobile."

"His car is worth nothing," the butler put in quickly. "A
heap of junk."

"A most unfortunate situation," Mr. Cutler said
sympathetically.

"Shall I remove the person from our property?" the butler
suggested.

Pepe's pent-up tension suddenly released itself in fury. "Dog!" he cried, jumping at the butler. "Do not interrupt when gentlemen are speaking!"

The alarmed butler retreated. His elbow, drawn back in defense, connected with the statuary on the bench, and in another second the pink angel lay among the stones.

With a cry almost of pain, Pepe leaped to the precious object. When he rose, it was with the left leg of the angel gripped in a shaking hand. "An act of heaven! Señor we are standing among the saints!" he cried, pressing it against his breast.

The horrified butler bent over the recumbent marble figure mumbling his apologies, pleading that the accident was Pepe's fault.

Mr. Cutler stood quietly, though not angrily, surveying the damage. "It looks rather final," he said. "In fact, damn final."

A wonderful thought now flashed through Pepe's brain. "Señor," he said, "from my Uncle Tito I know all about accident matters. This is not a total loss. You are very lucky, señor. In a grown man such a leg is worth five thousand dollars. In such a miserable angel as this—a mere *niño* which looks to have a pain in the stomach—it is worth, maybe, fifty. We will say fifty for the leg, señor, and you may keep it. For the rest of the body I will give you two hundred dollars." He pressed the two hundred dollars into the astonished Mr. Cutler's hand. "A fair settlement!" he cried. "You would go crazy with a one-legged angel in this garden, señor! I swear!"

Mr. Cutler worked his tiny mustaches with a finger knuckle. At last he risked speech. "Don't you feel that this amputated statue would be a travesty on your uncle's memory?" he asked. "Appropriate as it may appear."

"Travesty?" asked Pepe blankly.

"Something of a joke, I mean," Mr. Cutler said.

"A joke, señor?" Pepe beamed on him. "A joke was to my Uncle Tito like roses in June."

"Then it's a bargain." Mr. Cutler smiled, offering his hand. He indicated to the humiliated butler that he might help Mr. Monterey take the stone to his car.

"If you will come to Pico Street one day," Pepe said joyfully, "I will show you the time of your life!"

"I shall do that, surely," Mr. Cutler promised. "I hope you have a safe journey."

As Pepe rattled down the drive, the pink angel propped beside him in the seat, he waved back at Señor Cutler and the butler, at the stone lions and the branch-library house. "Señores!" he shouted. "Finish the sherry wine for Uncle Tito! Get plenty drunk, my friends!"

But in his brief elation Pepe had momentarily forgotten the lateness of the hour and the waiting María. They returned to him now with alarming and desperate urgency. A clock on top of a drive-in informed him that it was already ten-thirty. He pressed the gas pedal to the floor boards. With the ancient jalopy shivering in every part, he bore hard in the direction of Pico Street and the final resting place of Uncle Tito.

It was too late to retreat when he came upon the red police lights and stopped cars at the intersection of Pico and Sepulveda. With steaming radiator and a shudder of gears, he stopped with his nose but a foot from the scowling face of a traffic officer. There were many officers, the chrome of their cycles gleaming in the red spotlights. The badge on the officer beside Pepe looked as big as a tin washboard.

"This is a police block," the officer informed him. "Let's see your license."

Trembling, Pepe drew it from his billfold.

"Expired a year ago," the officer said, pulling his book from his pocket. He poked into the rear of the car. He rattled the spade and the crowbar and stared at the pink-marble angel. He shoved back his cap and wiped his brow. "Where you headed for?"

"The cemetery," Pepe explained timidly. "To my Uncle Tito, señor, if you please."

"Been drinking wine, huh?" The officer sniffed, then indicated the stone passenger beside Pepe. "Who's your one-legged friend?"

"It is for one who is dead," Pepe answered. "Señor, I am in a great hurry. If I could go now —"

"Go?" roared the officer. "Do you realize you're a hazard on the highway?"

"No, señor," Pepe protested. "People keep away from me. I have never run into anybody!"

"Hey, Pat!" shouted the officer to another, who was telling the next driver to run along. "Come here! I think I'm dreaming!"

"Señores," Pepe begged. "I am already two hours late. My María is waiting. If I could go now —"

The two officers told Pepe to get out. They made him walk the white line in the highway. Satisfied, they checked the brakes, which Pepe explained involved a matter of shifting gears and going into reverse if necessary.

"No taillight." The first officer wrote in his book. "No horn."

"No fenders and no bumpers," added the other.

With that, they moved the car to the side of the boulevard and added other things to the ticket. "Don't move this thing except with a tow car," the first officer said.

Up to now, Pepe had been cautious and patient, but when the officer called Pat demanded, "Whose yard did you dig this statue out of?" he broke under the strain.

In heated Spanish and remarkable English, he told them all he had been through. He showed them Mr. Cutler's name and address on the scrap of paper. He burst into tears trying to make them understand that if he did not get the headstone to the cemetery by midnight, Uncle Tito would see to it that every gringo in Southern California paid dearly. He waved Uncle Tito's letter under their noses. But all to no avail.

The first officer looked again at the spade and the crowbar. "Have you got a bill of sale or piece of paper on your angel pal there?" he asked.

"No, señor," Pepe admitted.

" 'One had a shovel, and the other had a hoe' " the officer hummed. "We'd better call the desk on on this, Pat, and have Flanagan check with this bird, Cutler."

"Good idea, Mac," the other agreed.

The first officer walked to his motorcycle. Pepe could see him talking into the radio mouthpiece. When he returned he thrust the traffic book into Pepe's hand. "Sign here!" he said.

"A thousand thanks!" Pepe said angrily, taking the ticket. "I hope you have a stinking New Year."

When the radio call was returned, the officer leaped for his motorcycle. He came back, scratching his head. "Flanagan says this Cutler character is on his way down here, Pat. No record and no warrant on Frijoles here." The officer called Pat shrugged, and went hastily away down the highway, where other cars were being stopped.

"I am saved!" Pepe cried. "Señor Cutler has told you!" But suddenly it came over him that Mr. Cutler had changed his mind, that he was coming to get back the pink angel. Maybe he wanted more compensation. "Señor . . . Officer Mac . . . is it all right for me to go now . . . yes?"

"You're not going anywhere!" Officer Mac growled gloomily.

When a long, powerful station wagon shot down upon them and Mr. Cutler stepped down from it, Pepe noted that Officer Mac's face grew longer. Mr. Cutler's little mustache bristled, and his hat was cocked over one eye. He produced cards and papers snapping them under the officer's nose.

"This Mexican is a friend of mine," he said crisply. "a very good friend. . . . Hello, Pepe." He waved. "These boys seem to have made a mistake of some kind."

"Wouldn't it be just my luck to flush a judge!" Officer Mac groaned. "But honest, judge, this guy is an insurance company's nightmare! He's—he's a hazard to life and limb! And this is a legal blockade!"

"You're telling me!" the judge said coolly. "I'm not questioning the condition of his vehicle, but he did not steal that piece of statuary. We'll leave the legality of police blockades to the Supreme Court."

"Yes, sir!" Officer Mac touched his cap respectfully.

"I take it, the . . . vehicle cannot be moved?" Judge Cutler asked.

"I'd suggest not, sir. Not without a tow car."

Judge Cutler waved him aside. "Put the angel here in the station wagon, Pepe!" he said. "Time is of the essence, as your Uncle Tito pointed out!" He consulted his watch. "Three quarters of an hour till midnight, Pepe. How about your girl friend, María?"

"Oh, señor," Pepe cried, "you are better than a million dollars!" He lugged the pink angel to the station wagon. "But María—Señor, María is a lost cause! My gardenias will be like fried apples by now, she is so hot at me."

"Maybe not," Judge Cutler said, as they whisked along. "Perhaps I can help you explain. A friend is sometimes useful in these things."

"Señor," Pepe said fervently, "you are one damn fine friend! But some things are impossible."

At the cemetery, Pepe carried the pink angel through the little gate and dropped it with a great sigh, planting it firmly upright on Uncle Tito's grave. His mission accomplished, he crossed himself devoutly, and with a gentle, affectionate laugh wished his uncle a happy New Year.

It lacked only ten minutes of midnight when they reached María's house. The gardenia corsage was, indeed, in tatters. And though all the rest of the Flores family were in bed, María still sat dressed in her best. It was apparent she had determined that if she could not see the old year out with Pepe, she would make no second choice.

"Oh, Pepe!" she cried. "Look at you! How could you?"

It was then that Pepe came to understand something of the eloquence that elevates men to the bench, and his respect for all things judicial and legal grew mightily. Judge Cutler had the gift of persuasion and the power to soothe. María softened under his courtly words, and sat entranced as the little gray mustaches twinkled and danced. "Pepe promised me the time of my life if I came to Pico Street." He smiled, beaming upon them both. "I can think of no better night for it."

As the bells rang and the whistles blew, María threw herself into Pepe's arms. She imprinted a firm kiss on Señor Cutler's cheek. They ate the cake, and had wine, and remembered Uncle Tito. To the judge's horror, Pepe tore up his traffic ticket and sprinkled it on María's hair.

"Now let's go!" Pepe cried. "Until you have seen a real Mexican party, señor, you have not lived!" In a moment more they were close in the station wagon, purring down Pico Street.

"Pepe," said the judge thoughtfully, "that was a remarkable accident we had in the garden tonight."

"It was nothing!" Pepe replied, warmly hugging María. "You should have known my Uncle Tito, señor. To him even the worst accident was a big joke."

Judge Cutler laughed happily. "I did," he said. "It just happened that I was the gringo who represented the railroad."

A HANDFUL OF BEANS

"One makes mistakes," my father sighs. "Our little Pedro is already ten years old. He needs a mother. If I had gone after Catalina years ago I might have brought her back. Is it not true, Luis?"

"If nobody made mistakes, there wouldn't even be a world," my uncle observes. "Nothing is perfect, José."

My uncle, who is Luis Gonzalez, sits on the floor, his back to the wall, with his feet stacked one upon the other. He is sighting through the notch between his toes at my father who is sorting dry beans on a newspaper in front of the stove.

"I should have made a fight," my father insists. "I should have killed the lettuce picker from Imperial Valley. Pedro's mother would still be here if I had killed him."

"It is not your nature to kill," Uncle Luis replies.

"A weak nature," my father sighs.

"A gentle nature which stays out of prisons," Uncle Luis corrects. "Do not punish yourself, José."

My father's hand moves among the white beans, but I think he does not see them. The fire from the stove makes black lines in his forehead. His cold cigarette hangs wet in his lips.

"A terrible mistake!" he cries. "What good is a house without a woman?"

He has been drinking all day, quietly and without pleasure. His hand moves again to the bottle beside him. Suddenly, he knocks it aside. The bottle rolls slowly across the room. The wine spreads on the boards.

My Uncle Luis moistens his lips with his tongue. "One's nature is one's fate," he says.

My father rises slowly, standing beside me. He looks around the one room of our house as if he is seeing it for the first time. He puts his hand on my head and rubs it back and forth. There is something he wants to say, but it is no use. The next moment he has taken his hat from the nail on the door.

My Uncle Luis puts both feet on the floor and is searching for his shoes.

"No, Luis," my father says. "Where I am going I must go alone." He steps quickly outside into the darkness.

I do not know whether to follow or not. When I start to move, Uncle Luis shakes his head.

"Keep on with the beans," he says. "There is much to be learned, even from little beans. With some you can tell good from bad right away. Others must first be put into water. A bad and hollow bean will float away. A good bean will settle to the bottom."

"Anybody knows that," I say.

"This life, she is a running water. You understand? We are all little beans."

"Where do you think Papa is going?" I ask.

"He is a good bean," he answers. "Perhaps he goes to burn a candle, or to buy more wine."

I work at the beans and remember the warm sunshine and the dry wind in the field when we laughed, following the harvesting machine with our buckets, picking up the fallen ones that escaped the sacks. It was only yesterday, out on Sepulveda Boulevard. It seems a very long time since then.

On the way home, my father observed that the weather would soon be cold and rainy here on the coast. "I wish sometimes I could go to the hot inland valleys of California," he sighed. Then he had fallen silent.

We knew he was thinking of my mother who is far away. Perhaps she is in the Imperial or Coachella valleys with the lettuce picker. By the time we were back home on Pico Street he had sold his bucket of beans to Señora Santee to buy wine. Since then he has not laughed or eaten food.

"Was my mamma a bad bean who floated away?" I ask.

My Uncle Luis makes a sausage end of his lips and scratches his ear.

"Such things are not so simple," he says finally. "You were a very little *niño* at that time. She was a very beautiful woman, that one. A woman who needed much love, like a date palm which is always thirsty for water. Her eyes wanted to see many things. She was like a kitten which can not be made to stay home."

"But not a very bad bean, was she, Uncle Luis?"

"I told you such things are not so simple," he repeats. "Remember about the running water. Sometimes when the current is very swift, even the good beans are swept away. You understand?"

His eyes are half closed in a sleepy smile. He taps his breast with meaning. "It is the mother you keep here which is important," he says. "She is the one who has everything."

"That's what Father Lomita says about God," I tell him.

"A mother—a God—" He shrugs. "What is the difference?" He makes a big yawn. "It has been said if one did not have a God he would soon invent one. Perhaps it is the same with a mother."

"Uncle Luis!" I cry.

But he has closed his eyes tight shut. A long breath whistles between his lips. He is asleep.

"Uncle Luis! I want to ask you something!"

It is no use. He is gone from me. I get up and cover his bare feet with my old sweater so they will keep warm. He is a man who can sleep on rocks. Even when he has just come home with a spare tire or a live chicken he has found, he can sleep. "An obedient conscience is better than Social Security," he says.

He is always saying things. They are sometimes a great worry to my papa and to Father Lomita. They have long arguments with him about what is a sin. Sometimes, it is a question of his influence on me, which is silly. My Uncle Luis would break a bottle over anybody's head who had a bad influence on me.

What is burning inside me is the thing he has just spoken. I have a mother somewhere, but she is not a real mother. I can not remember her. She is a good bean who has floated away.

It is possible to invent a real mother, I think.

It is like the night when my father pointed up to the stars. He showed me the Virgin Mother, holding the apples of paradise.

"But it is only a story," he said.

"Not if one looks hard enough," Uncle Luis corrected.

When I asked Father Lomita, he said the stars are what the hearts of people have made them. That both my father and Uncle Luis are right. Since then I have seen the Virgin Mother whenever I have looked.

I think now that I will invent my real mother. I will not always have to look for her anymore. I will not always be wondering if she has already come back to Pico Street, and if some pretty lady I have never seen before might be her. I will not be afraid she is somebody bad, or that she is in jail someplace with the lettuce picker.

I spell out her name on the floor with the white beans. CATALINA. It is a very beautiful name. She will give me good things like Carmelita Smith at the Caliente Café, and scold me like Señora Santee of the poultry store. She will tease me like Rosa Hondo, and swat me sometimes like Señora Cerrito in the grocery. If I am very good, she will kiss me. I will not have to wash my own clothes all the time.

In a little while I can see her as plain as anything. She is helping me with the beans. Her fingers are slim and brown, with many diamond rings. Her nails flash like little pink shells. Her hair is black and wavy. There is a smell from her like Father Lomita's garden. Her eyes are deep and dark and shining. When she smiles her lips are like the red leaves of the poinsettia. Her teeth are even whiter than those of Rosita Flores who is said to brush three times a day. She has a blouse of yellow silk, and a necklace of blue turquoise which is like my father's ring. Her dress is thin like fountain water in the sunshine. Her green shoes have little golden bows.

"What will we ever do with all these beautiful pearls?" she asks. They shower through her fingers and splash all over the newspaper. Suddenly, she is holding my face between her hands, laughing as she presses her nose to mine.

"They're just beans!" I cry. "Honest, they're just beans!"

My Uncle Luis makes a sound as if he has been struck with a nightstick. He has fallen sideways and hit his head on the orange crate at his elbow.

"Dog of misfortune!" he growls. "José, is that you?"

My mother has disappeared. I am so angry I could cry. I sit and stare at my Uncle Luis. His eyes are squeezed shut as he rubs his head.

"You better get yourself into bed," I tell him.

"Who was here?" he wants to know.

"Nobody."

"You were talking to somebody."

"I was talking to my mother."

He opens his eyes at me now. A heavy sigh blows through his nose.

"You were asleep, too," he says. "Dreaming. Come look at my head to see if there is blood where I hit."

When I have looked in his hair and found nothing, he slaps my pants and says it is time we both hit the sack. "Come, sleep in the bed with me tonight," he says.

"But what about Papa when he comes home?"

"Tonight he will not care where he sleeps." he replies.

I am not sure. My father always sleeps in the iron bed with Uncle Luis. Besides, I have a better place on the apple boxes which I have built into what Carmelita says is a no-good studio couch.

"We will put our two backs together. We will take a long trip someplace," Uncle Luis promises, as we undress. "Africa, maybe."

He wants to do a good thing. I can not say no. But I am afraid my mamma will not come near the iron bed with him snoring the way he does. It is a thing I can not tell him. But there is no way out.

When we are in bed, he grunts a pleasant goodnight. "I am going to shoot tigers," he says, "with a new gun I saw in a window on Wilshire Boulevard today."

When I do not answer, he asks, "Don't you want to shoot tigers, too?"

"No," I reply.

"I don't either," he sighs, "but it is better than shooting people."

He turns over, and soon he is making noises like an elephant I have seen washing himself with his nose.

I can not sleep. In a little while I slip out to my own bed on the apple boxes. I wait with my eyes open in the dark.

"Mamma—" I say softly.

I am sure she is there, if only I could see her.

"Don't you want to play with the pearls anymore?" I whisper.

But there is only the crackling of the stove which is cooling down, and the noise which is my Uncle Luis.

In the morning when I wake up, the coffee is boiling and my father stands at the stove. He has on a new blue coat which is the same color as the pants. His face is shaved. But his eyes say he has not slept all night. He is looking sadly at my Uncle Luis who is still in bed.

"A poker game?" Uncle Luis asks.

My father shakes his head.

"A suit of clothes is easily recognized," Uncle Luis reminds him. "Perhaps you helped a rich tourist who was too crocked to notice?"

"Nothing like that," my father says. He reaches into a cardboard box and throws my Uncle Luis a pair of grey pants. To me he brings a shiny leather jacket which is only worn enough to look right. It is a motorcycle jacket such as only happens to rich kids.

"A present for you," he says, and pats my cheek.

"Who gives us such presents?" my Uncle Luis demands.

"Father Lomita."

Uncle Luis drops the grey pants as if they are hot. "Charity!" he says darkly.

"A present," my father repeats. "A gift."

"Let the Padre give pants to people who need pants — not to me!"

"Still a good pair of pants, Luis," my father points out.

Uncle Luis shrugs. "It is man's nature to be ungrateful," he says. "But if it helps somebody to heaven to give away his old pants, I might as well do my part." He begins to pull on the pants.

"Last night it was impossible to refuse," my father says. "If we do not wear these things, the Padre will be disappointed."

"It's a miracle!" Uncle Luis exclaims, zipping up his front. "They fit!"

"Mine, too," my father replies. "The Padre has a good eye."

My own jacket fits like I am made for it. I know now where my father has been last night. But as he pours the coffee into our tin cups and we sit at breakfast, there is a big silence. My Uncle Luis is waiting to be told what he can not ask, and my father is thinking how to put it.

"A divorce is possible," he says finally, "but the Padre says a divorce is not the answer."

Uncle Luis nods.

"One must forgive," my father goes on. "One should wait. It is a matter of patience."

I watch as my Uncle Luis rolls a cigarette for my father and another for himself. My father blows out the match with a long breath.

"It will do no good for me to run after her now," he says.
"That is true, José."

"The Padre told me a story," my father goes on. "A poor man once dreamed that he had discovered the buried treasure of King Solomon. When he awoke in the morning he found a rare diamond clutched in his hand. He took this stone to a jeweler and had it set into a ring. He wore this ring on his finger all of his life. Wherever he went he was thought rich and was respected."

"A fortunate man," my Uncle Luis nods. "A story to remember."

My father smiles at me. "You are such a diamond, my little Pedro."

I do not know what to say to him. I want more than anything to tell him that I have seen my mother last night. That she was here in this room. When she went away I think she went to Father Lomita to put it into his head to give me the beautiful leather jacket and my father a new suit. She even thought of my Uncle Luis with the pair of pants.

"Someday you will understand," my father is saying. "Some treasures must stay buried forever." He stands up from the table and squares his shoulders. "I am going out to find a lawn to cut. It has been a long time since I felt like working."

"I will go with you for the walk," my Uncle Luis answers. "Pedro, too. It will do us all good."

"I can't," I say. "It is my day to wash my clothes. I must do my housework."

"A boy of character," Uncle Luis sighs. "A worker."

"A diamond," my father says gently.

As they leave, he gives me the little wave of his hand which means okay, keep out of trouble, he'll be back, and don't take any wooden nickels.

I have not said the whole truth. I want to go with them, but I want to be by myself, too. I want to tell my mother how much I like my new jacket. While I sweep out our house and wash the coffee cups and the plates from last night, I pretend that she is making our beds and picking up our dirty clothes from the corner to put into the wash tub.

More wood is necessary to heat water. I find I must make a trip to the alley behind Señora Cerrito's grocery store. It is a place where orange crates and lug boxes are to be found. This is not so easy. Señora Cerrito watches her boxes very carefully. Especially in the daytime. She is a handy one to swat little kids with sticky fingers.

But there is another way. My Uncle Luis has said that people should be given the opportunity to share their wealth before they are punished for being selfish. I think my mother would be proud of me if I walk up Pico Street in my new leather jacket. I think I should permit Señora Cerrito to make me a small present for the good of her soul.

The bell clangs on the rope when I go into her store by the front door. Chiquita Alvarado is there buying cheese. Señora Gonzaga, who is a grandmother five times already, stands feeling the tomatoes.

"Here is nothing to eat!" Señora Cerrito cries when she sees who I am. "Here is only work!" She is popping the string on Chiquita's cheese package. Her hands fly out and stay still in the air. "Where do you get this fine new jacket?" she demands.

"A present," I say, and shrug like my Uncle Luis when he is asked such things.

"And who gives such a present?" she inquires.

"Somebody," I say.

"I bet—somebody!" she snorts. "Somebody who laid it down for a second, maybe."

Already Chiquita Alvarado has her ears up. Señora Gonzaga comes to feel the leather. "It is not one from my kids," she says.

"Señora Cerrito," I say politely, "I need a small box to put a rabbit in. Perhaps an old apple crate—?"

"Rabbits!" she exclaims. "Such a jacket would cost new twenty dollars!" She studies me as if I am a mouse in a trap. "You want a box? You tell me first where you got the jacket."

It comes to me from no place like an itch in the hair. She thinks I am a thief! If I say my jacket is from Father Lomita she will not believe me. She will say I am hiding behind the Church. That it is an old excuse. In a minute she will try to skin my jacket off of me.

I stare into the glass case of bakery things to think. Suddenly, behind the glass, there is a face. It is the beautiful face of my mamma, and she is smiling to me not to be afraid. I remember that if it had not been for her maybe my papa would not have gone to Father Lomita last night. I would not have my jacket at all.

"It is from my mother," I say proudly. I look the Señora straight in the nose.

"Heaven preserve us!" she cries. She rolls her eyes at Señora Gonzaga as if it is the end of the world. "She wouldn't dare!"

"That Catalina!" Señora Gonzaga wheezes. "You think she has come back to José?"

"Impossible!" Señora Cerrito grabs my shoulder. "She sent this jacket to you? No?"

"No," I answer.

"Then she is here!" Señora Gonzaga shakes her head under her black shawl as if she is looking into a grave. "You have seen her?" she wants to know. "You have seen your mother?"

"Yes, Señora," I nod. "Last night. I have seen her, and she is very beautiful." It is no lie that I have seen my mother. But I do not say where.

"She's beautiful, allright!" Señora Cerrito exclaims with scorn. "Too beautiful. Poor José! She will be the death of him yet!"

"It figures," Chiquita Alvarado puts in. "This morning I passed him and Luis. He had on a nice blue suit. He was shaved for a change. It figures, allright!"

"Everybody must know!" Señora Gonzaga cries. "If Catalina is back again on Pico Street—" She spreads her hands to heaven.

Chiquita is already ahead of her, and holds the door open.

Señora Cerrito bends over me and squeezes my shoulders in her two strong hands. "You are like my own little son, Pedro. You come to Mamma Cerrito anytime you want something. You want a box for the rabbit, you take one." She pats my cheek. "Your mother — you think she will stay home now?"

I shrug. I do not want to talk to her anymore. "Please — may I have the box now?"

She waves me to the back door. She is standing with her chin in her hand at the telephone as I go out. I take two boxes.

On the way home I am stopped at Manuel Velez's barbershop. There is big talk going on.

"Five dollars says José will take her back!" Jesús Rinaldo, the gambler, is shouting as Manuel waves me into the shop. Then everything is quiet.

Manuel asks me about the two apple boxes I am carrying. I say I am going to catch a rabbit to keep in them.

"And how is everything at home?" he asks. "I have not seen José and Luis this morning yet. What is new with them?"

"My father has gone out to cut lawns," I say. "Uncle Luis, too."

"Of course," he nods, "but what is new with you?" He feels my leather jacket and clicks his tongue. "Besides the new jacket?" He winks. "Somebody pretty nice must have been at your house. How about it?"

"Maybe," I say carefully. "And what's new with you?"

"What a kid!" he laughs. "I hear you have company at home."

"Only our family," I say.

"I suppose," he says, "the family is still in bed asleep. No?"

"No," I say.

"Put up your five dollars!" Jesús Rinaldo repeats to Manuel.

I have but lifted my boxes to go when Manuel cries out to look in the street. A big blue station wagon is passing by. In the back is a great white object with my father and Uncle Luis squeezed in beside it. In the front seat is rich Mrs. Wellman who thinks nobody can cut her big lawn like my father when he is sober.

"What do you think of that?" Manuel demands.

"A little electric icebox," Pete Escobar says from the chair. "They are helping her take it someplace."

"What could make Luis lift an icebox?" Jesús Rinaldo demands.

They gang up on me as if I know all the answers.

"What gives with the icebox?" Manuel inquires.

I do not know any more than he does. It is better to look smart in such a case. "I'm not supposed to tell," I say.

"It is my experience that one of the first things a wife wants is an icebox," Pete Escobar says.

"Without money an icebox is impossible," Manuel replies.

"A wife can have money," suggests Jesús Rinaldo. He looks at me as if I am a slot machine which is about to pay off.

"I have to go catch my rabbit," I say. I pick up my boxes and march between them. They know if they put the heat on me too hard I will tell my father and Uncle Luis. They will be sorry.

The station wagon was going in the direction we live. I think maybe they will stop at our house so my Uncle Luis can sell Mrs. Wellman a dried starfish or some shells we have picked up at the ocean. My Uncle Luis can sell anything.

Our house is on the alley in back of a vacant lot. When I can see around the corner, the station wagon is there. Mrs. Wellman is standing beside it while my father and Uncle Luis are trying to pull the icebox from the back. I start to run, sliding to a stop when I am in front of them.

"Well, if it isn't little Pedro!" Mrs. Wellman exclaims. "José, he is becoming a more handsome child every day."

"*Gracias*, Señora," my father beams. "See, Pedro, what the Señora has given us. A fine icebox."

"Don't make so much of it, José," she says. "They wouldn't have given me much for it on a trade-in, you know. It was just the little one that Mr. Wellman used in the bar."

"She is very beautiful, Señora," my father answers. "She is just what we have always wanted."

Mrs. Wellman is looking around as if she is trying to find a bird in the eucalyptus tree. "But do you have any electricity here, José?" she asks.

My father looks to Uncle Luis. "Do you remember, Luis?"

"A detail," my Uncle Luis replies. "The wires, they are all underground, Señora."

"Of course," she says. "How stupid of me." But she keeps looking around as they are getting the icebox to the door.

"Would you care to come in?" my father asks with politeness.

"I'm sorry," she smiles, "but I have a hundred errands to do this morning. It was so nice of you to take the box off my hands, José."

She tells me I must come to see her sometimes when my papa is doing her lawn. Before we can understand how she has done it so fast, she is rolling away into Pico Street.

"You see, José!" Uncle Luis exclaims. "If I had not seen this fine box in time and warned her it is against the law to throw old iceboxes away without first taking off the doors, she would not have thought of giving it to us."

"But what will we do with it now?" my father asks.

"With such a box, who knows?" Uncle Luis laughs. "We can keep our beans in it."

While I help to lift, we carry the icebox into the house and place it between our beds.

My Uncle Luis plugs the electric cord into a knothole. My father stands rubbing his hand over the white enamel. "Luis," he says, "If Catalina had possessed such a fine thing as this, perhaps she would not have left me."

"One should not take a bath in the same water twice," Uncle Luis replies. "Perhaps Señora Wellman will throw away an electric stove, too, some day. We must watch for it."

At this moment I see through the window that Señora Gonzaga is passing in the alley. She peeps from under her black shawl. At the corner of Pico Street, Jesús Rinaldo is talking with Señor Santee, who sits in his poultry truck. Behind the fences and trees I see pieces of kids. They have been sent to learn what is going on.

I know I should tell my father what I have said in Señora Cerrito's grocery store and repeat what has been asked of me at Manuel Velez's barber shop. But I am afraid. Everybody on Pico Street thinks my mother is back and we are all dressed up, with a new icebox besides. I do not know how to prove that I have not told a great lie and brought trouble.

I shut my eyes and wish with my whole heart that my mamma will come into the room again like last night. That my father and Uncle Luis will see her too. *Perhaps*, I think, *if I touch the beans and make a prayer it will happen.*

I go to the bucket beside the stove and take a handful of beans and squeeze them until my fingers hurt. But nothing happens. Then I remember how she held up her hands and let the beautiful pearls rain through her fingers.

"Pearls!" I cry. "Look!" I throw the whole handful in a big shower over the white icebox.

"What does he mean?" my father asks in wonder. They both look at me as if I am out of my gourd.

Uncle Luis shrugs. "When the cork bobs, who knows what is biting the hook?" He gives me a long look and reaches his hand into the bucket. In a moment he has thrown a fistful of beans at the icebox. "A pleasant sound!" he shouts. "Try it, José!"

"Please, papa!" I beg.

With a great sadness on his face, my papa comes too. In a moment we are all throwing beans. They are bouncing from the white icebox all over everything.

At first we do not hear the loud knock. Then Father Lomita is standing in the open door, his knuckles raised to the wood.

"My children," he says, "This is, indeed, a strange sight."

I can not move. My hands are stuck in the bean bucket as if they are held in glue. My papa stands speechless. It is my Uncle Luis who turns a box on end and invites Father Lomita to be seated.

"The sound of beans on an icebox is like rain on a roof," Uncle Luis explains. "A beautiful sound in California, Padre. We are badly in need of rain."

"We are, indeed," Father Lomita says soberly. "There is much poetry in the sound, I grant you."

He stands very straight. There is no smile in his eyes as he looks sternly at our beds and the icebox and at the beans which are scattered everywhere. When his eyes fasten on me, I am ready to fall dead with fear.

"A certain matter has come to my ears," he says. "It is said that your wife has returned to you, José. Is this true?"

My father shakes his head. "No, Padre. It is still as I told you last night."

"It is said she has been seen in this house."

"It is untrue, Padre."

"It has not been more wine talking, perhaps?"

"I have not touched wine since last night," my father answers.

"Strange," Father Lomita sighs. "So many people are so sure." He sits down slowly upon the box. "Let us ask ourselves how such a rumor could start."

"We thank you for our new clothes," Uncle Luis says. "We have been given an old icebox by Mrs. Wellman. We have a few beans to eat this winter. It is a time of miracles. People talk."

"That does not help us, Luis," Father Lomita replies thoughtfully. "Yet you may be right. A strange thing happened last night. The clothes I gave José were left at the Church only an hour before he came to talk to me. There was

no name with the donation. They were just left. I wonder—?"
He looks a question at us all.

"Please, Father Lomita—" I say in terror.

"Yes, Pedro?"

"I—I am very happy for my new jacket." It is not what I
tried to say, and I am shivering all over.

"You are welcome, my child." His eyes rest on my face, and
I think he can see all the way into my soul. "It is said by people that your jacket was given to you by your mother. Is that
not a strange thing for people to say? Is it possible that your
mother has returned?"

I stare at the floor because I am full of shame.

My papa comes across the room and presses my cheek
against his side as he faces Father Lomita.

"You have taught us that the Church is our Holy Mother,"
he says. "Is it a lie to say this coat is from her?"

Father Lomita drops his eyes from my papa's face.

"That is the spiritual truth, José. But there is also a literal
truth which must be observed."

"How fine can you split a hair!" my Uncle Luis protests.

"And you, Luis. Do you know the truth of this matter?" the
Padre asks.

"I know that if a boy does not have a mother he will invent
one," my Uncle Luis replies. "Last night I have said as much
to Pedro. Perhaps, if I am the one who is at fault—"

Father Lomita lifts his hand for him to be still. He rises and
begins to walk back and forth as I have seen him many times
in his garden, rubbing his hair with his hand and moving his
lips as if he is whispering. Finally, he stops before me.

"God understands the inventions of our hearts better than
we do," he says. "We are all blind and stupid men, my child.
If you will tell us how everything happened, perhaps we can
better understand."

With my papa holding my shoulder and Father Lomita
looking away to the wall, I confess how I saw my mother last
night. About the beans which were like pearls. About what

happened this morning at Señora Cerrito's grocery store and in the barber shop.

Before I have finished, my papa is brushing his eyes with his sleeve, and Father Lomita has made a bad bird's nest of the rosary cupped in his long fingers. Only my Uncle Luis sits beaming upon me as if I am a shelf full of bottles.

"You are the love of my heart," he says.

"Pedro," Father Lomita asks, "do you remember at all how your real mother looked?"

"No, Padre."

"Catalina," my father whispers sadly. "She has been gone so long."

"José," Father Lomita goes on, "when you came to the Church last night, did you pray to the Holy Virgin?"

"Yes, Padre. I did."

Father Lomita kneels to the floor. He begins picking up beans, as he speaks to me.

"Pedro," he says, "you must keep some of these beans and bring them to me at the Church. We will make a Rosary of them. They are pearls of great price." he pours the handful he has gathered into my own hands.

"But they are just beans," I say. "there are lots of them."

"They are the blesséd food of the poor," he says. "Some-day you will understand. Someday they will be very precious to you."

We wait while his fingers move along his Rosary to the Cross. He holds it hard against his breast.

"What we have spoken of today is only between God and ourselves," he says, as he stands and blesses us. "Do not speak of it to others. Now, it is my part to set right the ears that knew not what they heard, and the tongues that knew not what they spoke."

He stops in the door looking back at me as if many things are moving in his mind.

"It is a precious thing to see a vision so clearly," he says. "A very precious thing. I want you, Pedro, to come often to my house. There is much we must talk over. We must think of what you will become when you are a grown-up man."

When he is gone, my papa paces the room without words until my Uncle Luis takes his arm.

"Perhaps," he says, "we can build a little shrine to the Holy Virgin inside our icebox. We will keep our beans there. Nobody would dare steal beans from before such a shrine."

"I will help," I say. I am already working to gather them from the floor.

"Yes," my father agrees, "we must pick up these blessèd beans. It must not be said that we are a family who live like pigs."